Duck Alley

by

Jim DeFilippi

THE PERMANENT PRESS
SAG HARBOR, NY 11963

F
Def

© 1999 by Jim DeFilippi

Library of Congress Cataloging-in-Publication Data

DeFilippi, Jim
    Duck Alley / by Jim DeFilippi
      p. cm.
    ISBN 1-57962-
    1. Title.
             1999

                        98-
                        CIP

THE PERMANENT PRESS
4170 Noyac Road
Sag Harbor, NY 11963

To Johnny,

the best brother there is

Also by Jim DeFilippi:

Blood Sugar

July 6, 1957, on the bulkhead:

"Hey, Tasti."
"What?"
"Let's do something. The both of us."
"Yeah, okay. There's nothing to do."
"C'mon, let's do it anyway. C'mon."
"What?"
"Huh?"
"Do what?"
"We hook down Cookie's house, c'mon."
"You mean like you said, with the chain? You really mean it?"
"Yeah. Let's. We'll get everybody, try it."
"You're nuts."
"Yeah. No. C'mon, let's."
"You're nuts."
"Yeah."

ONE

EXCEPT FOR FATE, it's kids themselves that are both the kindest and the cruelest of God's creations, often at the same time. What we once were seems to loom so much more radical and expansive than what we have become. During those early days our lives seemed to hold so much more drama and humor and tragedy. Yet we knew no enemies, we suffered no demons back then—not in the way we do now. No, back then there were only friends and non-entities, and both of these groups qualified for full doses of our kindness and our cruelty.

And it was a friend who would be the victim of our great, cruel plan.

Buster Cook was our neighborhood bum; every neighborhood had one. A sun-baked, scruffy, well-read man, in temperament and life style he was closer to us kids than to the grown-ups. He studied the dictionary and the *Daily News*, told us to do the same, and he knew batting averages. His skull had taken some shrapnel during what he called the Brown Shoe War and that was, our elders assured us, what made him the way he was.

Sometimes a new kid would make the mistake of referring to the metal in Cookie's head as a steel plate, like the one that Don Zimmer, the ballplayer, had inside of his. No, we would explain, there was only cooled and twisted shrapnel inside Cookie's head.

Cookie was a constant image on the streets and in the back yards of Duck Alley, as indelible as the blackened stain around an inkwell. He never worked a regular job, but he collected bottles and helped us mow the infield when it got too high to smack grounders. He would carve out straight and grid-even lines there in the scrub grass, underneath a red sun, using a borrowed hand-mower that would be clattering out its joy as it moved. He would mow the base paths an inch lower than the rest of the infield. Meanwhile we'd be off casing construction sites or Anderson's Greenhouse, trying to steal some red clay to build up the mound.

We all called him Cookie, but not to his face; he would chase you for that.

He lived in a junk-stuffed garage next to the train tracks, which is about where you would expect a guy like Cookie to be living. The garage had no square corners left to it; it sat on a forty by one-hundred lot that used to also hold a house, a structure which had long since dissolved down into just one cement foundation corner. No one owned the property, as far as we could tell—it was just Cookie's because Cookie lived there.

The long summer days were making us restless—a restlessness as intense as only a kid's on summer vacation can be—and it was this restlessness, along with the fertile mind of Albert Janos Niklozak, that first put the epic idea into our heads. It was an idea born of boredom and spirit, and the cruelty of youth.

My friend Albert Niklozak always seemed to be at the emotional center of anything significant that we kids did. He and his family were Hungarian immigrants and our grammar school, in the spirit of United Nations unity, collected money for their relatives back in Budapest during the anti-Communist uprising in 1957. What the money was to be used for was all sort of cloudy, but the television news was showing clips of simple, spirited peasants hurling Molotov cocktails at grumbling, growling, red-starred tanks. So we all handed over our Mite Box money each week with what we felt was equal spirit.

The entire Niklozak family was presented with a check at a ceremony out in the playground, right in front of the Blessed Virgin, who stood there smiling, still chapeaued from the May Crowning. Competition for May Queen had run particularly hot that spring; the fifth-grade girls would have slit each other's throats.

A rumor circulated that the Niklozaks ended up using our check to buy their first television set, but nothing ever came of the whole thing.

For a while before and a long time afterwards, Albert remained my friend of friends, a cornerstone of my daily excitement, one swell kid who happened to be peripherally enamored with bombs and munitions and any sort of armaments. That wasn't so unusual back then, not too long after Cookie's Brown Shoe War had ended.

It was Albert who first figured out the plan and then sold it to us. He had found a two-hundred foot long industrial cable with hooks the size of home plate welded onto each of its ends. He told us that he had found the cable wound up in a circle, lying fifty feet into the sewer tunnel that ran underneath the Third Hill. Albert and his dog had been seeing how far they could walk into the darkened tunnel without screaming and running back out. This was usually a group activity, but that day it had been just the dog and Albert.

The cable, an inch thick and peeling off rust like dried blood, was the kind of open-ended toy which by its very existence forced kids to be creative, forced those who were leaders to come up with an appropriate use for its size and strength and form.

So Albert did that.

Trains often stopped, for no perceptible reason, on the tracks right behind Cookie's garage. What we would do—Albert decided and we all agreed—would be to quietly loop the cable around Cookie's place, then hook one end of it onto itself, in this way encircling the garage. Then we'd wait for a train to stop, and we'd hook the other end onto the undercarriage of one of the cars.

We had all seen enough Abbott and Costello movies to visualize the results.

"But it's the guy's house for Christ sake, it's where he lives. We can't do that." Bobby Gallaga was often the counterweight to any plan that we'd come up with. "It's the

10

only place where the guy stays, for crying out loud. Don't be crazy. Don't be stupid." Gallaga—also called "Skull" or "The Giraffe," for forgotten reasons—seemed to exist just to punch holes in our schemes, very often using moral or ethical points as his weapons.

He grew up to join the Nassau County Liberal Party, and he ran for office every four years until his father's arrest record was made public by the Democratic County Supervisor's staff.

Albert's rebuttal to Gallaga's protest was simple, controlled, uncontestable. Letting the cable slide through his hand like a rosary, Albert explained to Gallaga and to us all, "So what, it's only Cookie." Incontrovertible.

Each of us agreed, Albert and Gallaga included, that Cookie would have to be out of the garage at the time of the hooking and hauling. We were hooligans, yes, but we were not man-slaughterers. That might come later in our lives, but not now.

There were about six of us, I think, waiting until nine-thirty the next morning, a time of day when Cookie was always at Barney and Rubin's paper store, reading headlines until Barney and Rubin flipped to see who would throw him out. We sent Gallaga to keep an eye on Cookie, to make sure that he didn't come back home early for some reason. He never did—Cookie's time management rivaled that of a guy with a job—but we just wanted to make sure.

Getting the cable hooked around the garage was a cinch; only our nervous giggles slowed us up. It was the waiting for a train to stop that took some time. A few of them slowed down, just to get our hopes up, but then chugged on.

Finally, at mid-morning, we managed to hook onto a temporarily immobile train heading in from out on the Island. Mostly it was passenger trains that came by, carrying guys in gray flannel suits into the city. But this one was a short string of maintenance cars—even better.

A metal ring was welded onto the understructure of the last boxcar, right behind the rear set of wheels. It looked like it had been designed just so kids could hook it up to a garage. It took two of us to lift the end of the cable and to hook it on. We waited in the bushes and agreed that this was so much better than squashing pennies on the track.

Somewhere deep within our communal conscience was the small festering thought of what we were really doing, that this was too mammoth a thing for kids like us. Still, we could no more tell ourselves as individuals to quit it than we could stand up and tell the group to quit it. Either act would involve too much loss of face, status, and image, the three sisters of preadolescent needs.

We were, after all, desperadoes waiting for a train.

Twenty minutes later, with the train still stalled, we were still crouched behind the clump-bushes of milk weed and punk, when Gallaga ran up in tears, spitting whispered words at us.

"Listen. Listen. Listen. Cookie's not at Barney and Rubin's. I looked all over for him all morning, he's nowheres around. Finally some guy said he thought he stayed home sick today. He was sick."

We could not look at each other. We looked instead out across the unmowed crabgrass that surrounded Cookie's garage. Each of us could feel the rest of us looking out there too. We didn't move and we didn't speak.

When the train blew a smokey whistle, we managed to turn our faces toward each other. I looked directly at Albert; he was looking at his dog.

All of us were about to go to jail for bum-killing.

Cookie was a guy who never fake-talked us like the grown-ups did, never shoveled us shit about how big we'd grown or what did you learn in school today. He talked to us for real, and he told us stuff that was worth knowing. Cookie was the one who first told me that everybody has to die. I don't remember how old I was at the time, but I remember it as big news. Very big. What could be bigger news than that? I was a dumb kid and this newly-introduced universal mortality didn't depress or scare me. I was just glad that I had found out. I was disappointed when I tried to share the magnificent secret with the rest of the world, and was mockingly made to realize that everybody else already knew.

Cookie could reveal marvelous and inspirational things to us. The four seasons followed each other—spring, summer, fall, winter— always all four of them, and always in the same exact order, every single year. I marveled at the symmetry of that and at the wisdom of a God who could come up with such a plan. Like I said—dumb kid.

We got older but Cookie did not age, and I was a shocked and embarrassed twelve-year-old the Thanksgiving morning that my grandmother announced to the family that Cookie was coming in to have turkey and lasagne with us. As far as I knew, Cookie had never been inside any of our houses.

My grandma said, "The poor man he stands in the street. All year he stands out there. He is not a dummy."

Cookie ate with us that holiday, self-conscious and silent, and stole a fat bottle of cheap Chianti as he was leaving.

On one hot afternoon when we were frying bugs with Mike Mahoney, Cookie shouted something to us from across Northern Boulevard, and Mike yelled back at him, "Shut up, Cookie." Mike yelled it just for fun, just for us to hear it and enjoy it. But Cookie squared up his shoulders toward our little group and took a step to the edge of the far curb.

"What did you say to me?"

We didn't answer him, just put our faces back down toward the bugs and the magnifying glass.

Then he was out into the street, still squared up at us, then halfway across. "What did you kids say? To me?" Traffic wasn't heavy on the Boulevard, but some cars were whizzing by. A black Kaiser had to swerve to avoid him.

Mike Mahoney looked to us for guidance. "Should I run?"

We all just told him, "Nah," and we watched Cookie from the sides of our eyes as we went back to the bug-burning. Cookie stood watching us for awhile, then lost interest.

Gallaga was sputtering at us, "You understand what I mean? Somebody said he stayed home."

Gallaga looked over at Cookie's garage. "Home. So you know where the hell he is, don't you? He's right the hell in there." Gallaga moved his chin out toward Cookie's home.

We reacted to those words and to the sound of the train getting ready to break inertia with the universal defense mechanism of youth— we ran. We ran in panic, that panic that can carry you over chainlink fences and fallen trees, past chained-up dogs, through traffic and back yards. A panic that doesn't let you feel the bloody blue-black knee or the scratched forearms or the pounding of the lungs until later on, when flight is over and the adrenaline is getting sopped up by your conscience-pumped blood.

By instinct we assembled on the bulkhead door behind the Donnos' house, and it was then that we, exhausted and hoarse with fear, and choking for breath, looked at each other and read in each of our eyes that we were cowards and back-stabbers and good-for-nothing killers of a bum.

My father was already an old man when I was growing up; he had been in his fifties when they had me, and whenever I think of him, he's sitting in the straight-backed chair on our closed-in back porch, pulled up close to the window that looked out onto our back yard. Pa would sit like that for hours. Smoking a Chesterfield down to its nub, sometimes leaning forward onto the old steam radiator case, sometimes nursing a stem glass of wine.

I imagined him seeing, from that window, everything that happened in Duck Alley.

We sat on the Donnos' bulkhead door and drew in deep breaths and I knew we were way out of sight of my father's back porch window, but I still worried about it, along with everything else.

It was then that somebody noticed that Albert wasn't there with us.

And we weren't about to go back to look for him either. Shame could be strong, but it couldn't quite drive us to move ourselves off that bulkhead. Instead we sat there listening for sirens and cop cars and screams and trains, but we heard nothing.

It was Albert who found us finally and, if we were to believe the tale that he told us, he was both the worst and the best of what we had to offer.

According to Albert, when we were running like the sniveling cowards that we were—although I myself insisted that I had never sniveled, not once—*he* had reacted with the valor of the Hungarian Freedom Fighter blood that ran in his veins.

His dog was named Sport but his nickname was Shadow because he followed Albert everywhere. The Shadow had followed Albert as he ran toward Cookie's garage. The dog had hesitated, then put his belly down into the grass and watched his master as Albert paused and then ran into the garage, looking to drag Cookie out. For some reason, Albert couldn't imagine Cookie walking out by himself. Albert also didn't think of unhooking the cable from the train.

He searched the rubble that was Cookie's interior design. Cartons and blankets and box springs and a free-standing closet. Unconnected bathtubs, a piece of a casket, the door of the old confessional from St. Mary's that the priests didn't need anymore. Unplugged refrigerators and a Dodge truck door, its window half down, and a rotted-out canoe—but Cookie wasn't anywhere around.

By now things were smearing together in Albert's mind, so he didn't know exactly how much time he had spent in the garage when he heard the train pulling out. He admitted to us that his Freedom Fighter blood thinned out just then, and he crumbled down into a ball on the cracked cement floor of the garage, lying there on a dried-up oil slick, holding the back of his head, wrists over ears, moaning. He heard the Shadow barking for him outside. He heard the moving metal of the train.

Some undetermined time later, with the train noise fading and Albert shaking, he pushed himself up and let himself know that he was still alive. With cold sweat drying on his t-shirt, he walked wax-legged from the garage and followed the cable toward the track. There he found its hook lying harmlessly in the gravel. The Shadow sniffed the spot; he too found no answers. A trainman, Albert decided, had seen the hook, flipped it off, and thus saved his life.

Albert stood awhile by the tracks realizing that he should be dead by now and that every day he lived from that point on was pure gravy.

Two days later, a cop driving a black Chevy squad car picked up Albert in his yard and drove over to Shelter Rock Road, where he parked and asked Albert about trains and chains and bums. We never figured out how the cops were brought into the whole thing. None of us ever suffered any consequences, because Albert would sooner give a hand job to a Communist than rat on a friend. If he told the cop anything at all, it would be based on denial, deceit, and unilateral action. Even back then, Albert's code for living was as solid and momentous as the Shelter Rock that the cop car was parked beside.

I took no life-lessons from our battle with the cabled garage. I wish I had. I wish that I had known then that the story of Cookie's garage could show me things about people and about happenings both tragic and noble. About the way some of us make our way through the world. And what we do to our friends, and what some of us will do *for* our friends.

Cookie never mentioned the train to us, but whenever he came around after that, he seemed to look at us a bit differently. And a rumor started up. Maybe I started it, I don't remember, but the rumor said that it was not a trainman who had detached the hook, but it had been Cookie himself. The rumor explained that Cookie had been wise to us all morning, and had been watching us just to see how far things would go, giggling quietly to himself as we were giggling to ourselves.

And the rumor said that the train had actually started to pull out when Cookie realized what was happening to Albert inside the garage, and Cookie had pushed his veteran legs hard to catch up to the train and flip off the hook without killing himself or getting his legs chopped off like that other bum had—that mythical bum who had fallen asleep drunk on the tracks somewhere out west.

Generally we didn't believe this tale about Cookie. But if that rumor were indeed true, then it was Cookie himself, the man-child of our little Promised Land, who had proven himself to be a bit cruel, as a child is cruel, but also noble and caring and kind, as only a child can be noble and caring and kind.

As only a friend can be noble and caring and kind.

August 18, 1955, on the ball field:

"Whoa, look this rock I found."

"Why should I?"

"Take a look at it. It's got a kind of a gold in it. Look at this here, the line there."

"Spit on it, see what happens."

"Pretty nice. Look. Gold."

"Yeah, it's something like that. Where'd you find it, because maybe there's a whole gold mine underneath us here."

"I rolled on it behind by third base by the foul line. Over there, when we got sick of rolling."

"Yeah, well, rolling's a stupid way to find a ball anyways. Why ain't nobody else helping us?"

"I don't know."

"Where's Gallaga? Where'd everybody go?"

"They went home, I guess."

"Shit them."

"Gallaga said he was getting poison ivy. He rolled over there by first, said don't go over there. He went home to wash it, said he didn't wanna get polio from it."

"That's stupid. The ball wasn't over there anyways. He was just rolling just to roll. Baseball's stupid. We gotta spend ten hours, weeds, every time to find the stupid ball."

"What'd they play in Hungary?"

"How should I know, I don't remember that. Baseball's stupid."

"They should have it, stupid rules, like, you keep playing with the ball after the cover comes off it. Like we do. You play with it unwinding it, you know, leave the string all over the base path. Wouldn't that be great? Guys getting choked and everything?"

"Yeah. And let's say you can't use a new ball till the old one's all gone."

"Yeah. Till you get to the little hard rubber ball inside. Then you throw it into the crowd, the ump does, then you get to use a new one. Crowd goes wild."

"You know what else? How about, if you wing it at a runner, you hit him, then he's out. If he's not on base. That would be so great. Smack, hit him in the back, hit him in the head, he's not only hurt, then he's out too."

"Yeah, yeah, what else? What else could we have?"

"What else?"

"I had one. A fan catches a ball on a fly, see, then you're out. Mickey hits one out, the fan, upper deck, he makes the play, you're out."

"God, there'd be a lot of fighting between the home and away fans. It be great. They could hire fans, the best fielders, let them in free."

"Great fan catches of history. Guy named Joe Forner caught Babe Ruth's sixtieth home run, you know. Joe Forner. That's true."

"Oh yeah? How do you know?"

"Oh yeah, I study this. I'm very good at remembering stuff, if it's stuff important to me. Forner. And it was a guy called Henry Diorio caught Ruth's last home run, but it was out in the street, so I don't know if you'd call Ruth out on that. I mean, it'd be tough for the umpire to see it, to call it."

"Diorio. Diorio."

"Henry. Nickname Wiggy."

"Wiggy. See, this way, with this rule, the fans would get as famous as the players."

"Yeah. Great. Best one was Reuben Berman though, Polo Grounds. Best fan catch in history."

"Willy Mays, he caught? Or Irvin?"

"Nah, a long time before that. Reuben-boy, he caught the ball, they wanted it back, see, like they used to back then, they wanted him to toss it back in, it was theirs, so Reuben he sued them for it. And he won, so the fans got to *keep the balls from then on. Yeah, he got to keep it. Changed the course of the game."*

"Wow. Shit. Absolutely changed how the game was played."

"Changed the whole entire history of the game, that's all."

TWO

THERE ARE TOO many starting points to chose from when trying to tell the whole story—good and bad—of me and my friend Albert Niklozak.

Some might trace our fall in life to those few decisive moments I spent with a girl named Arlynn Svenson in the hot and rolling sand dunes of West End Beach. West End was a high school and college kid-stuffed extension of Jones Beach State Park, which runs across the soggy bottom of Long Island.

I was in my twenties by then, teaching, already with a wife and kid of my own, but still feeling temporary about my promotion from the plastic and metal student desks, set in tidy rows, to the big wooden desk up front of the room. I still felt more like a member of the oppressed class than the oppressor, which is what I was now being paid to be.

Arlynn Svenson was a misguided senior with more breast than brain. I had been actively avoiding her when she caught up with me at West End and dropped herself down onto her knees there beside me on the blanket. She showed me her best pout, which was no more hooked into reality than was the daytime television world that she inhabited.

"You haven't been in your room after school," she complained to me. "I been coming for you."

I told her I'd been busy. I was trying not to look at her.

She leaned in. "Jay," she said to me, "Jay, I like how your lips go when you say 'Coochie.' Call me that."

I readjusted the weight on my elbow and I asked her how she was enjoying the trip so far.

She said, "Oh, okay, I guess. Okay, but I get a little bored sometimes. You know me. Always something."

"Yeah," I told her. "Yeah, well."

She leaned her head a bit down closer toward me. "How about you? I bet you get bored too sometimes, don't you?"

"Sometimes," I told her. "I guess so. Not much."

She waited awhile. She moved her eyes and then her hand across the sightline of the dunes and she pointed out to me how alone we were there.

I told her we'd better get heading back. Both the sun on my skin and the sand in my bathing suit had turned abrasive.

The top panel of her black bathing suit was held in place by two strings that were tied together behind her neck. Arlynn said to me, "Wait, before we go." Then, staring at me with sun-squinted eyes, she asked if I wanted to take a look at her. I told her we'd better not.

Her fingers were working the strings behind her head. "Come on. It's all right. I don't care. There's nobody here. Just look, that's all."

"Arlynn."

She started smiling at me and talking in her little-kid voice. Her hands came down from behind her neck. I was still propped on my elbow there on the beach blanket. I stayed still and I looked.

"Jiggle, jiggle."

She asked me in a whisper, baby-like, if I wanted to touch her a little bit.

I leaned forward to free my arm. Then my right hand had reached up toward her and stopped. I remember thinking that it was the same distance that God's fingers got to man's on the ceiling of the Sistine Chapel. Leaving open that little synapse of creation.

Arlynn called me a big silly and she kept talking baby talk to me.

I wonder sometimes, looking back at those two confused people there on the beach, how things would have turned out for the three of us—for me and Arlynn and for Albert Niklozak—if I had chosen the other path, the one less taken.

I wonder if the sinkage of our three lives could have been changed or avoided. Or would our interlocked crash-and-burn have happened just the same, with the three of us headed down, our arms akimbo and looped together, *apracet*, my grandmother would have called it in Italian.

I don't know. That is something I have never figured out.

But the story of the downfall of Jay Tasti and Albert Niklozak, and of Arlynn Svenson, did not begin there on the beach, with the sand and the lust scratching at the loins of a quick-warming schoolteacher.

No. In truth, to understand everything that happened to us as adults, and how much it all meant, you first have to understand how deep Albert and I went back. If our friendship were Yankee Stadium, we two would be rooted together out behind the monuments in center field, back when that grass and clay were still in play. It was that deep.

To explain things that happened later, I have to first try to show you about Duck Alley, the times back then, about the emotional equity that Albert and I had built up.

It was a world where all the bikes were J. C. Higgins, all the cereal was Kix.

If it's quiet and I listen—even today, after all that's happened—I can hear the sounds of back then.

Bazooka Joe, BB guns, Bungalow Bars if you'd missed the Good Humor Man. I'd pronounced his name, "Majooga Man." One Mississippi. Bruno Sammartino, Bobo Brazil, and azalea bushes. In school there were walkers and the bus kids, and you'd diagram sentences. Stick ball, stoop ball, punch ball, handball American or Chinese. Killing a snake by chucking dirt-bombs, a couple miles from where Gatsby's house would have been. Two Mississippi. Spaldeens and calling for a kid, hollering for him, to see if he could come out and play. Playing in the gutter, going to buy a Coke if you had the money after the Whifflle ball split and there was nothing to do. Drinking the Coke in a place that delivered your burger on a Lionel train, right to your stool, if you had the money. Three Mississippi. P.F. Flyers and Philco televisions, or black-and-white Dumonts, receiving and exhibiting their magic from atop rotted and deserted potato fields. Earl Scheib, for nineteen ninety nine, would paint any car, any color. Gee, Earl, you mean red don't cost more? A quarter for an Italian bread at King Kullen, a nickel for a Newsday, Dugan's home-delivery trucks and Krug's. A crippled beer man who could hold two cases and jump backward off the truck. Four Mississippi. A sling-shot was a Wham-o. You got your Wham-o? You bringing your Wham-o with you? Wetson's burgers and Grumman's—he works at Grumman's—what'd they do there?—don't know, something maybe with planes. You don't need an offensive line, because the defense they gotta count before they charge, count to five Mississippi.

It was a time before I knew that the things that we would do, and the things we didn't, would wreck the people that we knew so well, and those we hardly knew at all. It was a time when just hacking around was an acceptable way to waste away the day. Hacking around. Smoking some punk, guiltlessly burning up time, and when we were a few years older, burning both time and gasoline, just to do it.

Too often the forward inertia of our lives gets our focus stuck straight ahead, and we forget that everything we see before us is being illuminated, shadowed, colored and dis-torted by that mean-flashing light that is coming from behind our own shoulders. The not-real, jumping shadow that we see blurring black in front of us, confronting us, is our own head.

I figure that any story that is centered on good people getting crushed can only make sense if it's viewed with all of its pieces intact. At least that's how it finally came to make any sense to me.

The two of us, Albert and I, could talk for hours back then, looking for a baseball in the weeds, sitting on a stump, carving sticks into pistols, mopping up the blood from some small and appreciated boyhood wound. Just talking—bouncing words against the wall, using them to try to figure out how the world worked, always making things bigger and stranger and crazier than they really were.

Sometimes things were so nuts that we didn't have to build them up much at all, just remember them, and I was good at that. On August 17, 1957, Richie Ashburn, then with the Phillies, hit the same fan twice in one at-bat with foul balls. The first one busted her nose. Then Richie nailed her again as they were trying to get her out on a stretcher. How's that any less significant or impressive than Babe Ruth stepping out of the box in Chicago to call his own shot?

Albert was good at telling stories, and I could remember stuff. We could talk about things like Richie Ashburn so easily that it would be like talking to yourself.

There were other things that we couldn't talk about at all. And that turned out to be what was at the heart of our lives' misfortune.

Even today, things come up that would be interesting and funny to only two people in the world—to Albert and to me. Not too long ago someone said the name Nestor Shylock to me, I don't remember why. Albert would have remembered Nestor as an American League ump, 1950s. Sure, other kids who grew up then would have known the name too, but only Albert and I would have quick-jumped from there to another ump, Augie Donetelli, who we always called "Orgy" Donetelli, back at the age when that word was mysterious and dirty-thrilling and as funny as hell.

In some ways what I'm giving you will be a rose tinted mirage of those days tucked in behind Northern Boulevard, where match boxes and houses glow in sepia, where even the vanilla ice cream from the Good Humor Man will be slightly red-brown tinted.

Memory tends to be selective. I forget that for every time I came home to a house smelling of tomato sauce and baked bread, there would also be a time of smelling my grandma's *aglio e olio*, with its garlic and anchovy odor that would drive me and my uncles from the house. On those nights I would try to eat over at Albert's, hoping that they weren't having Naj Bimbaghulya's fish-head casserole.

My uncles used to call pork tenderloin "buffalo meat," and they would describe, during the meal, their mother's heroic efforts to slay the beast. *Pasta e fagioli* meant "pasta and beans," but my uncles pointed out, "If you ain't been to school, it's *pasta fazool*."

Albert and I had a lot, but in some way we didn't have much except for each other. I lived with my father, my grandmother, and her two sons, Uncle Rocco and Uncle Zippy. My mother had been younger than my dad, and she had gradually over the course of a few years just disappeared from the house and from our lives. She left me without a mother, but worse, without her stories. Like with Indians, it's the *stories* of an Italian-American that are a man's wealth—not his money, not his possessions—but his stories. My mother left me no stories.

My father remained a stranger to me and to the rest of the family. He took part-time and temporary jobs, quietly letting us know he hated each of them; he got old, and he sat alone on the back porch. Looking out at Duck Alley.

I had been given his name—Angelo Tasti, but the Junior on the end of it had been shortened to just "Jay" and flipped to the beginning. So to most people I was "Jay," but to Albert I was always just "Tasti."

Albert lived with his mother and father, and Uncle Frank before he died, and with Nagyneni "Naj" Bimbaghulya. All of them had been born in Hungary, but only Albert had been young enough to forget all that, to get on with his life over here as if Hungary had never happened.

Both of us an only child, both of us a bit askew from the world we lived in, content most summer afternoons just to sit on the curb of Brinkerhoff Lane, waiting for the ice cream truck, the edges of our Indian head nickels held so tightly in our fists that they would make an impression in the palm that would last for an hour. Nickels left deeper impressions than dimes did, and nickels represented ices, single-sticked, usually orange. Two more pennies would get you a double stick.

The dime bought real ice cream instead of cold, colored sugar water, but spending dimes for real ice cream was considered elitist.

The faces of those two kids waiting on the curb, faces ready to explode at the sound of the bell, still appear to me quite often, usually in that split second before sleep finally comes. They are faces without age lines or wrinkles, without the skin spots or booze-lines of now. They still manage to hold smiles of contentment and peace with the world. And, if I've been lucky enough so that the jagged edges of the world haven't made me too nervous that day, the faces even speak to me in lines of dialogue that I often won't understand until morning. And sometimes not even then. The words that they speak have been snatched out of the thin air of my history, from over-furnished back-porches of the past, where my father sat watching.

Pa was the Buddha of our back porch. Sometimes I figured that he was only checking the lawn—when it would have to be cut, where it had burned out, where it would have to be trimmed—and he wasn't staring at me or at Albert or at the other kids at all. But if he was just checking out the grass, that would be a terrible thing, and maybe it would be better that he died, as he did, before the things I'll tell you about happened to us.

Better he should have never seen Kevin Hoad throw a tuna fish sandwich at a car, or Rex Dooley get his head slammed against the basketball pole during Killer Ball, or me and Albert secretly sawing a limb off Whitney's tree to make the home run fence more accessible, and then each of us running home, struggling with the parameters of guilt and fate and bad fortune.

March 4, 1969, in the warehouse:

"Albert, you remember Buster Cook?"

"Yeah, Cookie the bum, of course I do, why not?"

"You ever think back to him at all, to back then?"

"No, what, of course not. Why should I? What am I, Emily Dickerson, I got nothing better to do here? Tasti, I ain't one of your fucking poets, I got a business to run here, got a million things I should be doing right now. This allows me the time to think back to bums? No, it does not."

"No, I just meant, I don't know, I think back. Sometimes. I was wondering, what do you think his real name was, anyway?"

"Who's real name?"

"Buster Cook's."

"Was Buster Cook."

"No, not his nickname, his real name, I wonder."

"Buster Cook. What are you talking about?"

"No, Albert, Buster's no real name. Buster. Buster's not real. It can only be a nickname. Believe me, there was no Saint Buster. Can't be a name, see?"

"Tasti, you fag-hole, there was never no Saint Jay neither. Never no Saint Tasti. You're sitting there, you're saying there's no name Buster. But it's sitting right there in front of you, for Christ sake. It exists, you're denying it. Cookie was Buster Cook. Buster. Buster. It's there. Try saying it. Buster. Use your fucking lips."

"It so happens, buddy, the name Buster, I happen to know, it all started with Buster Keaton. Which was just a nickname for him too. I know all this. Before Buster Keaton, there were no Busters."

"So Buster Crabbe?"

"Him too. Nickname. Came after."

"You're nuts. So before Oliver Hardy, you're telling me, there were no Olivers? C'mon."

"No, yeah, it's true."

"Before the Three Stooges, there was no the number three. Everybody had to go right from two, right up to four, skipping over."

"No, I mean it."

"So how'd they get Buster then, for Buster Keaton?"

"I think it was his parents used to bust him up. They were a vaudeville act or something, and he was a little baby, they used to throw him around on stage, drop him and stuff. And, I think it was, a 'buster' was a slang for when something got busted. They'd drop the poor kid on his head, somebody'd say, 'Jeez, that was a real buster.' I think that's how it was."

"You don't know."

"I know."

"You don't know. Except that part about being dropped on his head too much. That, I admit, that sounds to me like Cookie, all right. Good thing he had an iron plate in there from the war. That helped, but not much, not enough, I'm sure."

"Jeez, Albert, you forget so much. What's the matter with you? It wasn't a steel plate, it was just shrapnel in there in Cookie's head."

"Oh, right, there's a significant difference."

THREE

ARLYNN SVENSON, WHO was the catalyst of our destruction— Albert's and mine—and of her own, had taken my English 10 class in her sophomore year, then my American Lit the next year. She was the ultimate bad-news high school hanger-on—a pretty, thin-faced girl with an impressive body and more impressive troubles. She seemed to adopt me as her personal sounding board for absolutely everything that happened in her life, most of which never really happened at all.

She would hook onto me in the hallway between classes, or else come flouncing into my classroom at three o'clock. Then when she had me cornered and snagged, she would deliver endless, crudely-stitched monologues about things that she either believed or pretended to believe were her life.

Sometimes she would tell me about a group of girls who were waiting to beat her up. She was always vague about just what it was that had caused the animosity, and when I would walk her out of the building, there would be no one there. She would make a melodramatic show of checking the street and the parking lot for the thugs before venturing on.

In between classes, she'd be engulfed in some long, animated conversation on the hallway telephone down by the office; she'd allow hall walkers to overhear snatches of the best parts, the key phrases. But there was nobody on the other end of the line, just a dial tone and the poor kid's neurosis.

Sometimes she would tell me about a secret admirer that she hadn't seen in years—she was maybe fifteen at the time. Or sometimes there would be a guy that she had never met but that she would be having a first rendezvous with, that weekend. Her performances would key off scenes from her soap operas. Arlynn would do her best to imitate the actresses' horrors, and she'd do a terrible job of it. So what I had to witness or listen to, instead of heading home to my wife and little son, would be a bad imitation of a bad original performance.

These mystery guys of hers would always have exotic, romantic names—like Lars and Lon, never Eddie, never Vince. Once she told me about the new passion in her life. His name was Lard. She said to me, "Mr. Tasti, I looked into Lard's blue eyes and I knew that I would never be lonely again." The eyes of love, the eyes of Lard. Someday she might get to taste the lips of Lard. I looked at her, wishing I could switch channels.

More than a few of the students in the school were hyperactive, violent, anti-social, negative, and potential-wasting. But no one in the school could be more annoying than Arlynn. And no one had fewer friends.

She was one of the high school armies of one, strapping on loneliness like a companion, blaming only their surroundings for the situation, desperately hanging on for four years, then to begin the horrible cycle all over again, at college or work or maybe in the military. Facing a thousand more silent meals eaten in crowded halls.

Did I somehow encourage Arlynn's interest in me, during those times before our semi-tryst on the beach? I guess maybe I did. Was I a bit flattered, intrigued by the attention, a bit tingled down there where my legs met? Sure I was. Any high school teacher likes a student looking at him as he speaks. There's so little of it.

In the endless tales of her life, Arlynn would sometimes refer to herself as "Coochie Coo," as in "this little Coochie Coo." So I sometimes called her "Coochie," or "Cooch." Once I lied and told her that her face looked a little bit like Julie Christie's in *Dr. Zhivago.*

During her senior year I didn't have her in class but she would corral me and tell me of her plans to go to Hollywood after graduation to get into the movies. She had signed up for one of those scam teenage modeling courses, and she showed me pictures of herself posing in bathing suits and lingerie. I looked around the room and quickly handed the glossies back to her. I couldn't think of a thing to say.

She told me that she had missed out on her first professional modeling shoot—a bra and panty layout—because her aunt had come down with cancer the night before and Arlynn had to sit up with her.

That was Arlynn. If I were standing maybe six inches from the chalk board, and she was heading toward the window, she would squeeze through those six inches instead of using the rest of the room to get by.

I heard rumors from her classmates and my colleagues that Arlynn had a father or a stepfather who beat her up, but I didn't see any signs or secure any proof. And I never asked her about it. I tried never to ask her about anything. It encouraged her.

She found out the date of my wedding day and delivered an anniversary card for Annetta and me, using our first names in her message. She handed me the card while wearing a black sequinned dress and a black veil over her face. I never shared the card with my wife; I didn't tell her anything about Arlynn. Once, as the school was leaving for Thanksgiving break, Arlynn told me that she'd like to drop by my house. I told her not to, and I took nervous glances out the window during that Thanksgiving meal with my wife and child.

There had also been a nervous Thanksgiving meal years before, during that turkey dinner back in Duck Alley when my grandmother had invited Cookie in to join us. Grandma used to stitch the stuffing into the bird cavity like a surgeon, and a loosened string somehow got tangled around a button on Cookie's shirt sleeve as he was grabbing for gravy. Cookie's arm froze, then moved a bit. The big bird followed. Cookie locked the bird into his gaze, as if it were poised to attack him. The turkey jerked left, then right.

Cookie yanked and things spilled. My father deftly grabbed his overflowing plate of food, lifted it off the table, held it there like an offering. Uncle Zippy began poking the bird with a fork, shouting, "Back, Simba, back! Ah! Ay-aaaa!"

Uncle Rocko pretended to clear the room. "Poultry amuck here, folks, c'mon, nothing to see, move it along, show's over." He instructed Grandma to use a carving knife to cut off Cookie's button. Or maybe Cookie's hand.

Later, stuffed but still stunned, Cookie took leftovers wrapped in wax paper, put them into his hat, and left our house with the stolen Chianti—not a thank you, no good-byes.

Uncle Zippy explained to us, "Well, he probably doesn't say thank you to King Farouk either, when he goes over there for cognac and cigars."

A lot more turkeys had gone under the knife by the time I was in basic training and got a letter from Albert that read in part, "Did anyone tell you Cookie died? Yeah, finally. I was home and my mother made me go over there, clean out his garage/house. You know what I found? That Chianti bottle he stole from your family at Thanksgiving, you remember? On his shelf next to his Purple Heart and Vicks Vapor Rub. I'm sure it was it. There was a little wine still in it (it aged real bad though) and a date was put on the bas-ket with magic mark 11/24/55. I bet that was the date he copped the vino from you guys. What do you think?"

My Thanksgivings are quiet now—superfluous and carrying ghosts—and they clog my mind with memories of Thanksgivings past. Back then it was always a dining room table holding a model city made of foods. And swarms of relatives buzzing like locusts—voracious and destructive. Fat Joe would attend—a pseudo-relative at best, he'd been thrown out of the seminary on a gluttony charge. And the long Thursday afternoons would be dominated by the foolishness of those two bachelor boys of buffoonery—my Uncle Rocko and Uncle Zippy.

They were huge, curly-headed bookends who had developed their tandem sense of humor to a keenly adolescent level.

Just as Albert was fascinated by munitions, my uncles were fascinated by levitation. One year, right before the main course, as the turkey and myriad other dishes had been set out, they set themselves at opposite ends of the big dining room table and announced that it was time to contact the spirit world.

They closed their eyes, placed their palms down on the linen tablecloth and they pretended to enter a trance-like state. Lifting with their knees, they made the table rise and float a few inches in the air. The turkey platter and bowls and stuffing and potatoes were sliding precipitously, a few inches back and forth.

"The table moves," Uncle Zippy began to croon, his eyes still closed, his lips barely parted. "This is a sign that the spirit has entered the room. It's . . . it's . . . yes, it's *Compare* Biaggo, from Genoa, gone lo these many years. Speak to us, *Compare* Biaggo, speak to us."

Grandma and the other ladies sat with whitened knuckles held to their mouths, knowing it would be useless to try to halt the bogus seance. I was too stuffed full of antipasto and prosciutto with melon and minestrone and lasagna to worry about the turkey flipping over. I was more interested in how *Compare* Biaggo would speak to us, although he never did.

And so it was that Albert and I, inspired by my uncles' foolishness, tried to levitate Grandma herself one year. We didn't skimp on our choice of a floater. My grandma was big—short, but with a real "grenade-smothering" kind of body.

My uncles had come of age during World War II and had been in the Civil Air Patrol until their necks had gotten tired of looking up. They had seen every war film from *The Sands of Iwo Jima* to *Pork Chop Hill*, so they tended to rate people's bodies in terms of their grenade-smothering capabilities, since in every one of those movies someone hopped onto a live hand grenade to save the platoon. And their mom had a perfect grenade-smothering body—three-hundred pounds of love and digested pasta, much of it plucked directly from the boiling pot.

Albert and I had seated her in an overstuffed chair in the living room. The chair had spent its first few years in our house wrapped up in plastic, its next years actually being sat upon, its next wrestled on with friends, and finally used as a trampoline during the Ed Sullivan Show's circus acts.

Our hands encircled Grandma's body as if they were hummingbirds, detached and floating in the air. What happened next has always remained a bit unclear in Tasti family lore. Uncle Rocko, who witnessed the scene, insisted later that a metal spring had let loose and dug its ugly way upward into flesh.

Whatever the reason, Grandma's grenade-smothering body lifted out of the chair like a mortar shell. All present, as I remember it, including the uncles, fell backward in awe, shielding our eyes, as floor boards rumbled and creaked. Time stood still.

Later, the uncles decided that the spring pulling loose was not an act of coincidence but rather an act of Providence. They would tell you that they never again took the name of the Lord in vain, or gambled quarters on the hymnal numbers that the priest announced in church.

I used to have an entire repertoire of stories like that, to be performed at parties and in bars. When people would ask me if these tales of magic and enchantment and joy were true, I would just stuff my hands deep into my pockets and shrug my shoulders, corner-boy style, and ask them right back, "What do *you* think? I was there."

After Thanksgiving dinner, Uncle Zippy would explain to the crowd how it came to be that he had appeared in *Bridge on the River Kwai*. In reality, he had never gotten any closer to Hollywood than the Fulton Fish Market, where he worked at scale, but as the afternoon wore on—and various things were poured into the coffee—more and more of the relatives remembered seeing his face, until, by five o'clock, most of the grown-ups were in agreement that he had been the best thing in that movie—better even than the train wreck.

The years slowly robbed Uncle Zippy and Uncle Rocko of some of their showmanship, and I, with Albert's help, gradually tried to assume the responsibility for family entertainment, just as we had for the levitation. My best trick was putting my head on the bannister and then running full speed up the stairs until my head jammed between the railing and the ceiling. And Albert could do a yodelling Chinaman.

After the Thanksgiving meal, football would be on—it was always the Packers and the Lions back then—and at half-time I'd call for Albert and we would go out and toss the ball around. The smell of burning leaves hung in the air from a day-old burning, and there were always enough leaves still lying for us to pile up and leap into while making the catch and announcing the action. "McGee goes down ten, squares out, the ball's up, McGee dives, a great grab!"

Rogey McQuillen was not allowed to change out of his dress-up Thanksgiving clothes, so he had to watch the play from the street. He would stand there with a lost look on his face. I have seen that same look on professional athletes who are hurt and watching their team from the sidelines, leaning on crutches.

Once, during Thanksgiving grace, my father began to cry. I'd never seen that before and it puzzled me. He was drunk, but still. There, among the spilled cider and stupid jokes and carnival of relatives and talk of white meat and dark, my father—the statue of the porch window—had begun to cry.

Albert and I always argued over whose relatives were screwier. I had my Uncle Zippy and Uncle Rocko, but he had his Naj Bimbaghulya.

Albert and I were sitting in the Nazbeth movie theater, Saturday afternoon, waiting for the lights to gradually dim and the curtain to move and the kids to start screaming, when—in between gulping bites of popcorn—Albert first told me the tale of his Nagyneni "Naj" Bimbaghulya.

Naj Bimbaghulya was a semi-aunt of his who dressed like Whistler's Mother, could cook like Mamma Leone, and had a disposition like Ma Barker. Neither Albert's parents nor any other Niklozaks ever admitted any blood relationship to her. They all knew that she was Uncle Frank's wife, but that didn't help much since no one would vouch for him either.

Albert told me that Naj Bimbaghulya probably never was one-hundred percent all there, but the family traced her ultimate emotional decomposition to the episode of *Lassie* when Timmy had to give Lassie away to strangers. From that moment on, emotional overreaction became a way of life for Naj Bimbaghulya and, by extension, for all those who dealt with her.

She quickly developed a way of reacting to family situations that her allies described as "colorful," the rest of the family described as "nutty," and—according to Albert—her parole officer as, "That friggin' lunatic, get her out of my office."

Uncle Frank, he never said much of anything.

Things peaked when she managed to hide Uncle Frank away from the rest of the Niklozak family for a few years, even though he had passed away.

Albert finished off a fistful of movie popcorn, reached in for another and said to me, "Perhaps I should explain."

Apparently, Uncle Frank he kept his mouth shut and then he died. Awhile after he had gone to his final reward (although Albert pointed out that just getting away from Naj Bimbaghulya was reward enough for any man), things turned a bit strange. Naj Bimbaghulya's daughter Archanjela had offended her mother by getting thrown out of the Niklozak home at a very early age.

Archanjela compounded that insult when she told Naj Bimbaghulya that she had decided to get married and began to describe her betrothed to her mother. Naj Bimbaghulya objected to the poor guy on every point: American-born; young; outgoing and friendly; blond. Even worse than all of these traits, he was a bio-statistician. Naj Bimbaghulya felt that any career that she'd never heard of was probably illegal. She wanted Archanjela to marry a locksmith. It didn't matter which one.

When Archanjela insisted that her troth would be plied by the bio-statistician, and that it was *not* to be a locksmith who would be the one to unlock her flower, Naj Bimbaghulya bellowed into her daughter's face, "Go head, go you, you marry that bum. Dishonor you family. But you never see you papa's grave again."

And so, as Archanjela and the bio-statistician were exchanging vows, Naj Bimbaghulya was having Uncle Frank's remains disinterred with a back-hoe. In Albert's telling of the tale, for the next few years, the extended Niklozak family dedicated its free time to uncovering Uncle Frank's final resting place, which wasn't all that final since Naj Bimbaghulya kept moving him every couple months.

Archanjela lost interest in the chase after a year or so and she told her mother, "I don't care where you got Papa buried. He's in heaven."

"No, he's not," Naj Bimbaghulya answered her, "He was in the Blessed Rue, Row 57, Plot 2A up till last weekend. Now he's on the move again." And she went back to her ironing, smiling contentedly to herself.

Albert told me that the family tried bluffing the old lady, they tried elaborate four-car tails, nothing ever revealed the blessed locale.

Finally, on her deathbed, Naj Bimbaghulya motioned for her daughter to approach the railing of the hospital bed. Archanjela had to bend over close to her mother's tired lips in order to hear Naj Bimbaghulya's hoarse and whispered words. "I have but little time left on this earth. My final request of you, my only daughter, I wish to be buried next to my beloved husband."

"Fine, Ma," Archanjela answered, "so where's that?"

Naj Bimbaghulya opened her eyes one last time and said evenly, "Wouldn't you like to know."

"Albert, is any of that true?"

"What do *you* think? I was there."

With his tale of Naj Bimbaghulya completed, Albert went back to his popcorn. Then he twisted his neck around to look toward the projection room, hoping that move would bring about sooner the magic moment when the house lights leave and the screen is lit.

Eating and watching. Our two Saturday afternoon lusts. After every movie Albert could be found in the lobby, discussing the film and sucking his teeth.

It took five of us to convince him not to set off a bomb in the movie theater during an Audie Murphy. Disgruntled, he boasted that instead he would hit the screen from the balcony with a bone.

Albert was already respected for scaling flattened popcorn boxes and hurling apples cores great distances around the theater, but no one, we had to believe, could come close to hitting the screen from the balcony. With a bone. There were simply too many variables.

We frequented the stately Nazbeth movie theater, whose marquee was later used on the American Film Institute's letterhead, so this was no bandbox. This was a theater of considerable size and girth. It even had statues of little angels pissing in the lobby.

The entire Duck Alley gang was there, our collective breath held, on the day Albert would attempt to make good on his boast. Monk Capella, who was usually only allowed to watch the movie from the manager's office, had crawled under fifteen rows of seats while whispering, "Hide me from the usher."

As befitting a champion, Albert arrived late, with protocol and entourage. With immensely layered dignity, he took his center seat, front row of the balcony, and began eating the historic drumstick.

He ate through the Movietone News, then the coming attractions and cartoons, systematically picking the bone clean, his eating driven by hunger and aerodynamics. He munched coolly, slowly, almost casually, but insiders reported that he was feeling the pressure.

Finally, during an interminable love scene of the main feature—Van Johnson was involved—Albert slowly rose from his seat and loosened up his arm. Countless pairs of eyes squinted at him through the smoky darkness.

He studied the screen, as if looking in from the mound for the sign. His body rolled back. He kicked his front leg high up into the air like a right-handed Warren Spahn, drew his arm back behind his right ear, and he let fly the bone. Our eyes followed as it arched beautifully, spinning like a majorette's baton, and it slammed into Van's three-foot-long earlobe. A small rip or grease smudge was punched into the screen.

The crowd went nuts. Confused ushers fanned out down the aisles like Gestapo. They knew the crowd would not react like this to Van kissing some dame. It sounded more like the time Vinnie Price got what was coming to him in *House of Wax*.

Albert stood, waving regally to the crowd from his balcony, cupping his hand away from them, Italian style. Neither the Pope nor Mussolini were ever held in higher esteem by their masses.

Like a chicken bone hurtling toward a movie screen, our best times were special to us mainly because they held absolutely no sense of truth or logic at their core. We were becoming familiar with the truth-saturated logic of the adult world, and we were not impressed. The only things that mattered, the only things that we planned out and executed, had to have neither foot—that of truth nor of logic—planted on solid ground.

The nuns taught us that there were seven Holy Days of Obligation. We felt that *no* day should be a day of obligation and, if there were any holy days at all, they were Christmas, Thanksgiving, Saturday, baseball, and April Fools.

Our best April Fools Day was April 1, 1961, a Saturday sitting on the outer edge of our simpler times. John Kennedy was in the White House, blossoming under the weight brought about by elective office. Albert and I were blossoming on the buoyancy brought about by our having secured our junior driver's licenses.

We decided to devote the entire first day of April to gags. The only criterion was that the gags had to make absolutely no sense to anyone, including ourselves. We considered many plans—but if we could explain 'em, we junked 'em.

We spent the morning in Albert's father's car, a two-tone blue '51 Plymouth we called the "Fleet" because of its hood ornament.

I was at the wheel and Albert—being shorter—was in the trunk, which was closed down but not locked. I would pull out onto a quiet, two-lane road, driving slowly, and I'd wait for a car to start tailgating.

When one did, I'd knock a knuckle on the black metal of the dashboard, right above where the radio would have been if Albert's father had ordered one as an option. In the trunk, Albert would hear my knock and he'd flip open the trunk lid. He'd be sitting there on a small wooden crate. Eating a cheese sandwich. He would pause, mid-bite, look back out at the tailgater as if he were an interloper, then go back to eating the sandwich.

After allowing a proper time for this to transpire, I would pull the Fleet off to the roadside and stop. The tailgater would sometimes slow up to see what was going on.

Straight-faced, I'd get out of the car, go back around to the trunk, slam it down hard with Albert ducking just in time—and I'd drive off.

When we tired of this, we drove the Fleet out to Jones Beach. No one was swimming yet, but there were plenty of walkers, mostly older folks, on the boardwalk and along the beach front.

We had slipped into our matching gray, tweed, ankle-length overcoats that we had found in a trunk in Albert's cellar. We called them our Nikolai Lenin coats and we wore them only for very special events of revolution.

When we got to a spot on the beach with a maximum number of onlookers, we and our Nikolai Lenin coats walked slowly into the water. It was bitter cold but we walked into the breaking surf without breaking stride or breaking into grins. Once beyond the breakers, our progress was easier. We kept walking until the Atlantic Ocean covered the tops of our heads.

I had read about the suicide of Virginia Woolf in English class that year, but I hadn't taken it seriously.

Later, we dried out and warmed up with supper. Then, as it was getting dark, we put on our still damp overcoats, grabbed a kerosene lantern and, along with Albert's dog Shadow, we went over to dig holes in Wick Rapp's back yard.

When nobody came out, we fired a couple Roman candles over Wick's roof. Old Lady Rapp came out and chased us, so we shot off the rest of the candles and a few sky-rockets over a cliff on Nazbeth Bay.

It was dark by then. We just slugged around on the rocks, me and Albert and his dog, watching the fireworks burn out above the bay.

Albert's adult frame closed out at a height of only five-foot six, but he had at least six-foot, six-inches of vein-lined muscle and wiry sinew packed into that plug of a body. As he grew, his childhood love of bombs and munitions partially mutated itself into an accent on blood, iron pumping, confrontation, and just-below-the-surface violence.

For his entire senior year, he never went out on a date wearing a shirt. Warm weather it was bare-chested, cold it was a windbreaker over flesh. A tough guy, Albert always tried to grin as he was vomiting. It was said that he once gave blood just an hour before a Golden Gloves bout, just to even things up. I think this particular part of the legend somehow got Albert confused with Muggs McGinnis of the East Side Kids.

I can, however, vouch for the fact that as Commissioner and star running-back of the Clapham Avenue Tackle Football League, Albert lobbied hard to play the games right on the concrete and gravel of Clapham Avenue itself, instead of on grass and dirt.

Later, when I had gone off day-hopping to Saint John's and Albert was starting up in business, he told me that there was no knuckle-action for him around the old places. So, when struck by the old urges, he had been reduced to putting on a propeller-topped beanie and going into Queens to walk strange neighborhoods after dark.

For awhile in high school, Albert had tried to drag me along on his street-fighting excursions, but I begged off, explaining to him that between all the blood and tomato

43

sauce, I wouldn't have enough clean white shirts for school everyday.

The truth was that I just didn't have any stomach for fighting. After a fight was over, I couldn't get the images of blood and bone out of my head—strangers' faces, red-eyed, mouths covered by fingers leaking blood. Albert understood how I felt about it, and he just let it go.

Arlynn Svenson finessed me into a physical confrontation with a student of mine named Buddy Lewis. Piecing the story together later, I realized that what must have happened is that Arlynn had lured the poor, dumb muscle-head into the girls bathroom right next to my classroom.

She had let him get a few of her top buttons undone, and then started screaming and banging on the wall. I was the first teacher to get there and I had Buddy pinned up against the side of a stall, my forearm across his neck, my face and ears burning with righteous anger, when help arrived.

The kid tried to sputter an explanation to me as I held onto his upper arm and walked him down to the office. Later, I told the principal that the cops should get involved. Mr. McCardy took off his eyeglasses, took a deep breath, and told me I'd do well to steer away from Arlynn Svenson. I asked him what the hell he meant by that. He told me, just do it.

That week, two or three fellow teachers told me the same thing, in one way or another. I had to consider it.

Both Albert and I got drafted during Vietnam, but only Albert served in combat.

Only once did I get him to talk about Nam—he called it S.E.A., for Southeast Asia. He was home on leave, stationed stateside on a little California post, doing TDY—temporary duty—in the motor pool, counting the days until discharge. Getting short.

We were in the Cave, an old bar hangout from high school; we were drinking quarter drafts. Albert told me some stories—like about a friend of his, an airborne, who was parachuting into enemy fire when the other jumpers' chutes all started taking off back up into the sky like rockets. The guy finally realized—it's not *them* taking off, asshole, it's you falling.

Only an auxiliary chute allowed this guy to survive his story.

There is a line in a Bob Dylan song about "emptying the ashtrays on a whole other level." Sitting there in the Cave, drinking, listening, I could tell that's what Albert was doing about Vietnam. There was a whole other level of what had happened to him over there, unspeakables that had damaged him and people he knew. He held his mouth a little different now, didn't move his lips as much when he spoke. Still, most of him was the same guy I had driven to the induction center a few years before. So if he wanted to tell Vietnam to me as a place of laughs, a place where Uncle Rocko and Uncle Zippy and Naj Bimbaghulya would have fit right in, then he had that right.

We kept drinking the drafts and reminded ourselves of the first time we had snuck into the Cave for a beer. We were seniors in high school, packing fake I.D.'s and flashing disdain for convention. We met a couple girls who told us they were in college, so we told them we were in college too. Since none of the four of us ever mentioned any names of institutions of higher learning, there were doubts all around.

They stood us up the next afternoon and, in order to remove the stains that their perfidy had put on our egos, we decided to buy some hard liquor at the package store.

We selected Beefeaters gin, because we liked the picture of the limey with the big hat on the bottle; but we hated the taste. We managed to choke down a half quart between us and found ourselves sitting on the sands out at Jones Beach. We both were wearing our Nikolai Lenin overcoats and we vaguely remembered walking down the boardwalk at the main beach sprinkling sand from our oversized pockets like it was magic pixie dust.

Near-sick, we sat there in the cold sand, felt the sun going down behind us, and we watched the ocean turning black.

"What'd we do with the rest of the Beefeaters?"

"We got much left?"

"Still about half."

"Christ."

Finishing it off was beyond us—if we did, we'd surely see it again, coming back up. Pouring it out into the sand would be too wasteful—we were sure there were kids throughout Europe and China dying for a pop of British gin. So we formed our hands into claws and we began digging a hole about two feet deep, right off the edge of the board-walk, at the corner. We would bury the treasure, come back and dig it up sometime later when we were in need.

I had a terrific lay teacher in English that year who had begun to make me see how things were connected, how everything could come together with power and signifi-cance. So, as I reached into the hole in the sand to gently place the Beefeaters at the bottom, I asked my friend, "Albert, what is the symbolism of this?"

In turn he asked me: "Huh?"

"What is the significance, the symbolism of this act?"

His drunken, bewildered stare burned into my face; he obviously thought it was the greatest single question anyone could ever ask. With his blank eyes aiming directly into mine, Albert said to me, "Nothing, I guess."

He thought some more about the symbolism of it all and kept his face motionless as he shook his head and repeated to me, quite solemnly, "Nothing at all. I don't know."

In the old war movies, William Bendix would turn to say something to a comrade, forgetting that the guy had taken a bullet on the beach and was no longer there.

Sometimes an indistinct sound, or a shadow across the corner of my eye, or a piece of a song on the oldies station, will make me turn toward Albert like that.

October 14, 1953, in the schoolyard:

"Hey, kid. Kid. You a girl or a boy?"
"Boy."
"Why your hair like that?"
"I don't know."
"How come you're out here?"
"The Sister tell me."
"Sister Edelina told you? You got kicked out?"
"Hm."
"Yeah, she's a jerk. She kicks me out too, but it's rain-ing. I thought they didn't let her do it in the rain though."
"You kicked out too?"
"Now? No, but sometimes I am. Not now. It's in the rain. I just had to go home because of my father. I gotta go back in. You should tell Father Maeo, in Confession or something, she made you stand out here in the rain. If you get sick and die, it's her fault."
"Hm."
"She's so fat she don't get wet, but you could die out here. I hope you do. Serve her right."
"Yah."
"I saw you out in the hall before I went home. You're new, right?"
"Yah."
"Don't say 'Yah,' like a jerk, say 'Yeah.' You moved into the Breathwaits, huh?"
"No."
"Yeah. Didn't you move into on Fourth Street? Y'know, Fourth Street?"
"I think so."
"You did, because I saw you. I live on Brinkerhoff, right up from there."

"Ah."

"I heard you're a Commie, right? You one of them Rosenbergs? You from Russia or somewhere?"

"No, from Hungary, a long time ago. We come here from Astoria."

"Where's that, in Russia? You're a Commie."

"No, not a Communist. We against the Communists. We hate them."

"Oh, yeah. That's good. What's you name?"

"Albert."

"How long you been here, just today?"

"No."

"How come Edelina threw you out?"

"I ate the chalk."

"You eat chalk? You jerk, how come?"

"Hm. I don't know."

"Usually for something like that Edelina would just punch you in the back. She probably really hates you. She hates Commies anyway."

"I don't know."

"How come you're such a jerk you ate chalk?"

"I don't know. Some kid said to."

"Oh, some kid? Oh, Richard Barnes, right? He tell you to?"

"I don't know."

"He's the big kid, with the plaid jacket, real, real dumb."

"Yah."

"Yeah, that's him all right. Hey, he can't even read. Yeah, well, don't listen to him. Tell him to go get lost. Tell him you're gonna break his glasses. Tell him about the time he threw up the Holy Communion on himself. He's a jerk. He's not gonna make you do anything you don't wanna do."

"Okay. Next time."

"Sure. Yeah, that jerk Richard Barnes used to try to mess around with me too. Now, no. He tries it with everybody. Just don't let him."

"Okay then. Thank you."

"Well, I gotta go in, see Edelina. I'll see you later. Don't get too wet out here."

"Okay. What's you name?"

"Tasti. Don't get wet."

"Okay, Tasti."

"Go get a hair cut, for crying out loud. Go to Pete's. I could show you."

"Okay."

"Watch him though. He's blind, so he clips your ears."

"Okay."

"What you got in your hand? Lemme see it."

"Chalk. See?"

"Jeez, it's all wet and everything."

"Uh-huh."

"Cripe, look, it's gumming all over your hand. It's all coming apart, like paste."

"I been holding it."

"Yeah. Hey, I don't know, listen, Albert, you think you and me oughta try eating it some? What'd you say?"

"Yeah, okay."

FOUR

WE WERE SITTING in a shack we had built on land belonging to Albert's uncle, upstate New York. The Shadow, now ancient in dog years, was asleep and twitching in a corner. We'd come north for the killing.

We sat and thought back to how the dog had been with us the spring day we took apart the brick wall in Mrs. Camilla's back yard, back in Duck Alley. The years and the moisture had busted up the wall into ugly, useless chunks and Mrs. Camilla told us that she wanted it out of there. So we got shovels from Albert's and we searched my garage for a couple old, drop-forged, eight-pound sledgehammers from my Uncle Rocko.

Then the three of us—Albert and me and the dog,—headed over to Mrs. Camilla's and the dead wall.

Albert had gone back to his house to get a red-handled pick that he had stolen off a landscaper's truck. He used it to root around the rotted base of the wall. Then we each took one of the sledgehammers and started pounding hell out of the bricks and mortar. A couple times Albert pretended to slam his foot, just for a gag. Hopping around like Gabby Hayes.

The work was hard and we'd switch sides every few minutes, just for a change. Albert took off his shirt. We'd stop to pry away at the bottom of the wall with the noses of the shovels, using the action as an excuse to put down the hammers for awhile. The dog would move in to sniff the cracks we were making, or try his tongue on the sweat drops that had flown from our arms. Then he'd back off, maybe chew on a chunk of bark or a busted brick.

After a time the pain in our upper arms and shoulders turned dull, and we found a rhythm in our hammer swinging, pretending we were circus roustabouts or railroad coolies. Neighbors, used to the sound of garbage trucks and sirens, would have to stop and try to figure out what the sound of such a rhythm was.

My father had watched us work from his back porch window. I looked up at him a few times, but I didn't wave.

The dog, tired of hunkering down and watching our mechanical movements, wandered off. He'd start barking now and then, not like he was onto something, more like he was just checking in with us.

We sat in the shack upstate and we talked about that time.

Albert never got any medals for Vietnam; and our combined war experiences never did cause us to grow up, any more than Cookie's train or college or working did. If growing up meant getting cynical about the world, Albert was already grown as a child, and I'd have a few years left of my childhood.

In a way, both Albert and I grew up one year after I was discharged. That was when we were in the shack that we called a camp, up by Newburgh in Orange County, New York. Up there with Albert's dog.

We remembered all of that—about Mrs. Camilla's brick wall and about the dog and the military—as we were sitting in the camp that we had built ourselves, weekends, with lumber and nails scrounged and stolen from down on Long Island. A bottle of Bellows Partners Choice stood between us on the table. We were using plastic cups.

That November had been cold and gray, sadder looking than most. The dog was awake now, restless, slow, just moving around the little room.

I poured from the bottle and then used my fingertips to slide it across the table before I stood up. I stood there a minute, waiting, but Albert just took a sip and kept on talking. He didn't stand.

He was talking about the time we had gone hunting almost up by Canada. The dog had come too, even though he was no good as a retriever or anything, even back then.

His name, Scout, was just a joke. He was no scout, he was just a shadow.

A guy that Albert's mother worked with had shown up to go with us on that hunting trip. Her idea. Christ, remember that guy? He was sporting about five-hundred bucks worth of catalogue outfitter clothes. Camouflage pants and waders and a jacket with loops for shells and aviator sunglasses and even a compass and a Swiss Army knife. Sweet stuff.

Albert and I had looked at each other. The Shadow had sniffed around the guy like the mother ship had just landed from Mars. That afternoon, the dog pissed on the guy's leather cartridge pouch.

We didn't laugh about it until later.

We laughed about it again now, and we both looked over at the dog. I sat back down.

Albert and I were both able to carry and preserve part of our youth through and beyond Vietnam. All the churning things that were connected with that war forced the rest of the country to push their extended fingers into the whirling fan-blade of reality. But not us.

Albert stood up, opened the front of the wood stove, slipped in a log, used the poker to shuffle things up a bit. The dog watched him. Albert looked at the dog, then he sat back down.

Yeah, maybe the rest of the country had been chopped apart by the war, but not Albert, and not me. It had been tougher for him, of course, getting introduced to people gunning for his death, while I was typing up I.D. cards in Alaska, afterwards telling people I was a "Vietnam *era* vet," using a cough or hiccup or my palm to disguise the middle word of the phrase.

Every time Albert got back from the army on leave, he wondered if the old dog would remember him. The dog would always manage a leap on its old legs and Albert would get a lick to the face. When Albert had come home for good, discharged and still alive, he said the dog's leap had been a little higher, the lick to the face a bit wetter. As if the dog knew.

Now, there in the shack upstate, the dog was sniffing the door to the closet. He stood there pointing his nose at the molding of the door frame. It was a corner closet that we had built the summer after we put up the camp. The closet was made to hold rifles and shotguns, rain gear and empties.

"No, Scout, you dumb bastard," Albert called over, "that's no door there, it's a closet."

The dog moved away.

Albert pursed his lips to give me a resigned sort of look. I moved my head a bit, agreeing. Albert stood up.

As the dog had matured, he had become scared of things in the world. As a puppy, he never used to mind the thunder. But once he was grown up, you'd leave him chained on the porch and you'd come back after a summer storm, he'd be sitting in the living room, still chained to the porch rail, his chain draped through the ripped-out screen door.

He'd be feeling bad, you could tell. Albert would slap his nose, hard, and show him the ripped-out screen, and Albert would make his voice into a growl and ask the dog, "What's this? Scout, what the hell is this? What's this?"

The dog would curl his tail into his ass and he'd feel bad. Then he'd do it again the next time we forgot to let him in for a storm.

As he got older, the dog finally found a way of overcoming his fear of thunder. He went deaf. Too bad in a way, because throughout his whole life, he had held complete confidence in each of his senses. He'd be sleeping in the yard and a passenger jet would fly over at thirty-thousand feet. The dog would lift his head and sniff at it to check it out—who was aboard, did he know anybody, stuff like that. Then he'd put his head back down, go back to sleep.

He always recognized good food from bad, and people food as the best, but he ate everything.

And now in his old age, more and more he recognized

pain. Arthritis. Sometimes Albert would untie him just to let him run off his suffering. But it just made it worse.

The dog had a place to go when he was hurt or scared— the basement of a high-ranch that had never gotten finished because the developer had run out of money. Sport hated that man, growled at him just for being around, but the dirt cellar of the man's financial project was the place Sport had to be sometimes. Like the time the car had hit him.

Whining and whimpering and licking his side and feeling more guilty than anything else, somehow putting his owner's anger before his pain. In his own little high-ranch basement.

He had tried to run off there this morning, before the three of us had taken the drive off the Island up to the shack.

Now the dog was over by the window, staring at the wall below it, maybe thinking that it was the door. I could see where he had worked away the hair on his hot spots. He kept his nose at the base of the wall below the window.

"Dumb as a dumb shit, and deaf, and now blind too," Albert said. His dog.

I answered him, "Yeah."

Albert kept standing. I didn't move, so Albert sat back down and pulled the bottle across the table top. It was a wobbly table that we had made from the two-by-fours left over from the porch.

Albert had stood up the same way an hour earlier, but then we had started talking about the fat goalie playing boot hockey on Loed's Pond, and about June's Beach, and about the time we had worked a hot summer week cutting firewood out of a swamp by Nazbeth Bay.

It was chain saws jumping octaves as we worked, and cigars, and too many bugs. Pay was five bucks an hour and a six-pack each afternoon. The dog would hang around, disappear for a half hour, come back, flush a bird, and then disappear again.

We both remembered a dog biting a nun once. On her foot. Had that been Scout or was it Scout's mother? Neither of us could remember now.

Albert pushed the bottle over toward me.

Finally, he clicked twice at the dog and yelled, "Get away from that damn window." His voice was sudden and it was too loud. "Come on over here."

Albert slapped the side of his pants. "C'mon. Here."

The dog could only get his back quarters part way across the room. He lay down in two stages, a grunting of pain coming from somewhere deep inside him after each stage. He rolled onto his side on the floor, his eyes open. One eye was a little bigger than the other.

Albert grabbed the bottle, took the last from it, and then leaned out, put it down on the floor next to the dog.

"Look," Albert asked me finally, "did we come up here to kill a dog or not?"

"Yeah," I answered him, "we come to kill a dog."

Our whiskey ballet was over.

Now both of us stood up.

❖

July 13, 1965, on the patio:

"Hello?"

"Yeah, hey, Tasti, it's me."

"Whoa, Albert, where are you?"

"Where am I? Where you think I am? I'm down here in basic, you jerk. I'm down here getting up at five o'clock in the morning in the dark so you can be home, sleeping in safety. We just got a patio break."

"A what?"

"They give us a patio break. It's forty guys in fatigue pants and issue t-shirts standing on a slab of cement. Out here in the hot sun."

"Oh, yeah?"

"Sure. What we do is, for fifteen minutes we're all just out here smoking, and pissin'n'moanin, and we work the word 'fuck' into our conversations as much as possible. We got three telephone booths, they're all lined up ten deep. Everybody's calling home, it's nuts here."

"Hey, sounds pretty awful, soldier."

"You kidding me? It's the greatest thing happened to us all week, maybe since we got here. Patio breaks are like being delivered unto heaven for five minutes. Listen, I don't got much time, I got fifteen guys pounding on the booth for me to hang up."

"Fuck 'em."

"Oh, you'd fit right in down here."

"So what's basic like?"

"You'll find out soon enough. They don't only draft dumb Hungarian aliens like myself, you know, they take natural born American fags too."

"Yeah, I know. I'm on my way."

"Yeah well, I'll keep a bunk warm for you. But it ain't so bad. It's just stupid, that's all. They're bouncing quarters on your bed and messing with your foot locker. They keep you running twenty hours a day and yell at you the rest of the time. It's all an act."

"Yeah?"

"We had K.P. from four in the morning till after midnight. It's not bad, just stupid. You'll see."

"Yeah, in two weeks I will."

"Listen, Tasti, I gotta go, they're going nuts here, for my booth. Do me a favor, will ya? Call up my Ma, tell her I don't need the money order for the plane ticket. They take care of it all here. Tell her all the other stuff too, I mean all the crap about how I love her and shit, my regards."

"You didn't call her up yourself?"

"What? Nah, I got no time. I got no dime."

"What'd you call ME for?"

"Huh?"

"What'd you call me for, you didn't call your own mother? What'd you want?"

"Nothing. No real message or anything. I guess, I don't know, I guess I just wanted to talk to you, tell you don't worry about it."

"Yeah."

"Nah, I just wanted to hear from you, that's all. You don't write, you cocksucker. I just wanted to hear from you."

"Yeah."

"Yeah."

FIVE

ALBERT AND I once had one of those conversations that didn't mean much to me at the time—just two corner boys shooting the shit— but as I looked back at it later, bathed in the light of the stuff that had happened to us, it made the palms of my hands itch.

He told me that John Profumo should have taken care of things with Christine Keeler. He had been a big shot in English politics, got caught with his Doc hanging out.

Albert told me, "Woman like that, just a pussy looking for some bad news, screwing up his life like that, you take care of it, before it gets in the way of everything."

"What'd you mean," I asked him, "'take care of things'?"

"You take care of things, that's all," he said to me, "before it screws you all up. A woman, you know, they can do that, if a guy doesn't watch his own ass close enough."

At the time I just let it go—Albert being Albert. Later on, I wasn't so sure.

After Duck Alley and Vietnam and taking the dog upstate, Albert and I didn't see too much of each other for awhile. He seemed to be having an easier time than I was leaving stuff behind and getting on with this business of pending—or pretending—adulthood. He seemed to be more able to see everything that came after Duck Alley as simply an extension of those early times—with the gags maybe a little more elaborate, the scams a bit more dangerous, the scars slashed into the skin a bit deeper—but still all of it based on nothing that made much sense except for action and belief.

I tended to look at the future as a new place; I reasoned it to be duller, more depressing, a hell of a lot scarier, and much too busy. All at the same time.

Albert used his Nam veteran benefits to go to Nassau Community College for about three weeks before dropping out because of parking problems around the campus. He turned a nice profit on the text book and tuition assistance imbursement, which he never handed back in.

Before the army he had started driving a truck for the Yacovazzi Brothers, a storage company with tentative ties to one of the New York families—somebody said it was the Bonannos. He went back to that when he got out, but we all knew that Albert was too smart to be driving a truck for long. I worried about him. I knew that he could take care of himself; I just hoped he wouldn't try to take care of himself *too* much, and wind up somehow getting nailed for it.

Springs and summers he kept busy in his spare time smuggling and selling illegal fireworks that he was bringing down from upstate.

After my early out from the service, I went back to Saint John's and graduated with a B.A. in English and couldn't find work. Albert told me that the drop-outs like him had taken all the jobs. I decided to go back to grad school and get a teaching license.

I got into Long Island University—summers and weekends I dug graves for tuition and spending money. We didn't actually dig the graves by hand—a Polish guy called Hack sitting on a backhoe did that work. But the bucket would leave the bottom of the hole scooped out on a curve that wouldn't permit the box to sit all the way down in.

So a kid named Billy—who was older than me but still considered a kid by everyone—and I would hop down into the six-foot pit with our shovels and our work gloves and we'd trim out each grave, making the four corners as sharp and as straight as an architect's blueprint. They called it "boxing it up."

Someone caught Billy down in one of the new holes playing with himself, and soon his infamy outran his performance. Just seeing him down a hole was enough to start a new story. It got so bad for the poor kid that whenever anyone came upon Billy working, he'd look up, pleading at the grinning face, "I ain't doing nothing, honest. I'm working." He'd hold up his shovel, gripping it with both hands.

When we were done boxing the hole, we would scatter a few rocks and pebbles on the bottom so that we could work loose the straps that would lower the box down after all the mourners were gone. For five hundred bucks, you could get a cement vault around the casket, to keep the worms out.

I remember standing hunched behind some hedges and watching the regulars disinter an Indian. They wouldn't let us kids in on the action, but we wanted to see. The Indian's wife was relocating to Florida and she wanted to have her chief down there with her. As I watched, the iron teeth on the bucket of the backhoe accidentally cracked through into the casket. Everyone slid a little closer to take a look. I come up to within a few yards, stretching my neck to see.

All that was left of the poor Indian was his suit and his bones. I always figured that the scene would have made a good television commercial for Robert Hall, or for whoever the guy's clothier was. You may be long gone, but your bones and your suit live on.

Whenever I'd talk to Albert about my job, he'd ask me to keep an eye out for Naj Bimbaghulya's Uncle Frank. I worked at that graveyard for about a year and never spotted the once-missing corpse of Uncle Frank the whole time, even though I'd catch myself looking for him every once in awhile.

Grave digging actually appealed to me, but not to my reputation, so when Albert called to say that he had dug up something better for me, I told him I was interested. I still had a semester and part of a summer to go to get my teaching degree. I had talked my way out of having to student-teach.

By then Albert had moved out of the trucks and he was helping run one of the warehouses that the Yacovazzis used in connection with the hijacking branch of their enterprise.

He got me a job working stock in the place. It offered better money, a chance to be around stolen stuff, and an opportunity to fool around on the forklifts.

The work was easy—brief periods of hard labor surrounded by hours of waiting for the trucks to come in.

There was a girl about our age named Annetta who was working paper there in the front offices. I knew that Albert had gotten her into the place too. Some guy in the back tried to tell me that Annetta was a fairly easy mark, but I didn't believe him. The guy was a jerk, and Annetta was completely compelling.

She was almost tall, and almost thin around her hips and seat, with dark features and olive skin. Her nose hooked a bit—I saw it as more Roman than Jewish—and her eyes were very round and deep—dog-brown. Her lips curved down at each end, even when she was smiling. Her teeth were large and flat across the front, with bulging canines—a look that I had always found very sexy.

She had an appearance that most people would classify as "ain't nothing special," maybe even tilted a bit toward the homely side. But the idea of people thinking of this remarkable woman that way made me love her looks even more.

I volunteered so many times to take invoices up to the front office, up to Annetta's desk, that the other stockies stopped teasing me about it.

A couple weeks into my employment, Annetta and I were standing, kissing, in a hidden back corner of the warehouse between the military-green metal shelving and the industrial-gray walls. It was late afternoon and the trucks were all in, most people were gone. Annetta was making short little noises of enjoyment as I kept kissing her.

I separated our bodies to an angle so that I could begin handling her. My cupped hand went down and I began using the heel of the hand and my fingers to knead her there.

She didn't stop me and she took my face in both of her hands as we kissed.

Only when I tried to lift her dress up, grabbing handfuls of the light cotton and trying to lift it above her thighs, did she gently touch the back of my hand to stay me.

But we kept on kissing.

A few weeks later, I took her to the movies to see *The Lion In Winter*, then to Wetson's for fifteen-cent hamburgers, and later she guided me lovingly through her night.

The next September, right before I was scheduled to start a teaching job in Levittown, we got married.

Albert was our best man.

Both of us knew that I was going into this thing in the same way we used to fool around while driving the Fleet— with both eyes shut tight. At least at those times Albert would be sitting shotgun, telling me which way to steer and how fast to go. And we never hit anything.

But at the wedding Albert gave me no advice or hints at all. For his toast he said that Annetta and I should go out to dinner at least once a week—her on Wednesdays, me on Fridays.

The reception presented him with at least three opportunities to knuckle some of Annetta's drunk cousins, but, in deference to us and to the occasion, Albert kept his fists in his tuxedo pants pockets that day.

That night, in a darkened motel room in Connecticut, my bride stood at the foot of our bed, her body back-lit by the television screen. Her flimsy nightie barely made it to the top of her long legs. She was eating a lemon-filled Dunkin' Donut, with her teeth slicing off little circles of dough and cream, her tongue cleaning up around her lips and chin. I would never be more ready for married life.

I never told Annetta about my flirtation with Arlynn Svenson. A day after I had dragged Buddy Lewis off

Arlynn in the upstairs girls room, she had invited me into the same room, probably using the same words that she had scripted out for Buddy. I thought about it. My guess was that she would not have started yelling for help—as she had with Buddy—but that she would have let me finish whatever I felt like finishing. It was after school, about three-thirty. The place cleared out pretty fast.

I stood there telling myself I'd better start recognizing trouble once it hammers me in the face three or four times with a frying pan and a piece of forbidden skin.

Arlynn stood up very straight, inviting, her breasts pointing up and her fingernails splayed out across the wood of the girls-room door like blood stars. I said to her, "Well, let me take a look at you here, Cooch, let me see about this. Quite a proposition here." Me smiling, enjoying the moment, trying to sound like Uncle Ben in *Death of a Salesman*.

Arlynn was smiling back at me. Something about her always reminded me of a thinner Petunia Pig, Porky's girl. That wasn't necessarily a bad thing.

Suddenly, the empty hallway filled with the sound of the cavalry from a Randolph Scott western. It was the thundering hooves of the boys track team. When it was raining out, they ran their laps inside, up one hall, down the other. Most of them—running and breathing hard in their sweat shirts and gym shorts—didn't even look at Arlynn or me as they rumbled past.

I told Arlynn to get on home and I ran from her approach from that moment until the time we met again in the dunes of West End Beach.

Albert broke away from his direct relationship with the Yacovazzi Brothers, somehow managing not to get his knees broken in the process. Not too long after that, he had his own place, a prepubescent fencing warehouse sitting just outside of the old neighborhood. He was doing well after a brief start-up period, and he was quietly proud of his success.

In some ways, Albert's warehouse and storefront became an adult extension of Duck Alley. The place was an echoing, L-shaped cinder block building that always smelled of cigars and Lysol and ten-year-old stories. The building was ten-thousand square foot, almost every inch of it covered with stock left over from Albert's last deal and corner-boys left over from the nineteen-fifties.

Billy Devereaux, an old Duck Alley rock, had sliced back his sideburns and was subletting a corner of the place from Albert to deal Volkswagen bug parts. Bobby Gallaga, who had panicked us years before when he told us Cookie wasn't down at the paper store and was probably at home in his cable-wrapped garage, dropped by a couple times a month. A runt named Mockie Sciaca came in every weekday for the whole day to sit and drink Sanka and smoke his White Owls and let everyone watch his hair fall out.

The stories around the coffee urn always concerned old dogs and gruesome nuns and short-pants adventures of years gone by.

Back in high school, Mockie used to have trouble getting anyone's attention, so he had developed a killer nipple-pinch. You'd be standing in the hallway when a debilitating pain would jolt out across your chest. You'd look down and there'd be Mockie, grinning and trying to start up a conversation.

We all told him he was a pervert, that he should be doing this to girls instead. Albert once nailed him so hard that his body dented in a locker door on its way down.

But now it was Time itself that was nipple-pinching the guys in the warehouse, trying to get their attention to tell them to finish up their breakfast and get on with their lives. They were all doing their best to ignore the message.

If the story of the guys in the warehouse were made into a low-budget horror movie, like the ones we used to see back on Saturday afternoons with chicken bones and popcorn, the movie would be called *The Time Warp Zombies*.

I saw Time Warp Zombies all the time around Duck Alley and in Levittown, where I was teaching. And they never failed to make me sad. You know them too. The Time Warp Zombies are the guys who get out of high school, but never really leave it. To this very day they can be seen at the parks and in the bars and alongside the school baseball games. They're telling stories of their high school years and remembering every score, and every play, and every gag and every party, but little else.

As the sun sets on the town, the Time Warp Zombies can be seen on the street corners, their empty eyes staring at nothing, their empty heads trying to remember what once was there. Year after year they stand like that, getting bald and bloated, talking about what used to be, but never mentioning what could have been.

Every time we talked about Biff in *Death of a Salesman* in my American Lit class, I stopped and warned the students about a fate such as that. Whether you were a high school sports star or a hallway queen, there's no glory in the past without a steady look to the future. And it doesn't just happen to the queens and to the all-stars. It's anybody who hates what's happening, but still can't break away from the roots.

Roots could be okay. The roots that we had in Duck Alley could hold us and protect us and sustain us. But those roots ended up grabbing us and entangling and choking us and enslaving us, just as the Time Warp Zombies had been grabbed and entangled, choked and enslaved.

There was, of course, a magic word that could have freed us from the clutches of these hypnotic roots. And that magic word was *good-bye*. Say it and we'd be free. A magic word, but not an easy word to say.

I never did.

Sure I had gotten on with my life in some ways. I had a decent job in another town, a wife, plans for a career and a house and a family. My body didn't get sucked back into the warehouse more than a couple times a month. But my mind was back there and on the streets of Duck Alley a lot of the time. Still is.

So, even as I wasn't sitting shooting the shit with the guys at Albert's warehouse, I had to look at myself and admit that, yes, I too had fallen under the spell of the Time Warp Zombies.

Albert had yanked himself free of the spell because, even though it was *his* place that was the meeting place for the old crew, it was also his money-maker, and a good one. The Yacovazzi Brothers still took a percentage of every-thing Albert dealt—from pillows to wigs, electronics to chewing gum, plumbing supplies to dentist drills. On some deals the Brothers got a flat fee, off the top, plus their cut each month. Albert was smart enough not to buck *that* trend, but there was still enough business to keep him in business, to get him his "three squares and a flop" each day, as he would describe it.

At least seventy percent of the stuff he was dealing from the warehouse was legit, with real bills of sale and owner's manuals and even warranties. Stuff Albert had bought below wholesale or taken on consignment from the local dealers. The rest of the stuff, Albert liked to say, had been acquired by the "midnight re-route"— the trucker had turned east, the stuff turned west.

This was the stuff he'd fix up by changing the serial numbers, ripping out labels, restyling, re-tooling, making up phoney bills of sale, re-stumping cashed checks, and lying a lot, straight-faced.

Albert was a smart businessman, and he knew enough about human nature to keep people thinking that everything in the place was swag. People just liked to buy stuff that they figured was boosted. They'd even pay more for the privilege.

From seven to nine each morning Albert would take in merchandise from the boosters. These guys were little more than shoplifters, but in a much larger sense than we ourselves had been shoplifters as kids. We used to steal candy, twenty-nine cent toys, cigarettes by the pack.

These shine-thieves were up all night going after television sets, canoes, and cigarettes by the truckload.

In addition to the warehouse, Albert kept a list of drops—blind pigs—both floating and permanent ones, around the North Shore. He processed the more high profile stuff through the drops, until it cooled. He also did all of his fireworks business through the drops, rarely if ever on the premises.

Gallaga told me that Albert was also dealing firearms—small handguns mostly—but I never caught a true indication of that. It could have been, I don't know.

Albert was the perfect proprietor for the place. He could look at an offer and know exactly how much he could get for it. He'd be dealing for a hot load with one hand, cooling a mark with the other. And smiling and talking, same time. Really enjoying himself.

He tried to keep everybody happy, including the Yacovazzis and the man. Cops were always welcome in the place, made to feel at home. He'd only offer them deals, gifts, or bribes when he was sure it would not embarrass them.

But he couldn't please everyone. A young, ambitious assistant district attorney named Ron Cloud Carlini started going after Albert pretty hard. Ron Cloud referred to him as Albert "Nickels" Niklozak, as if he were a mobster, and Ron Cloud tried to bring in indictments on fencing, prostitution and shylocking. "That jerk," Albert said to me, "I never once shylocked in my entire life."

Ron Cloud finally managed to get one of his indictments to stick with the grand jury. Albert was allegedly found to be in possession of a truckload of plastic wind-up mobiles that you would hang on a baby's crib. The case went to court, where Ron Cloud had to prove that the mobiles had indeed been stolen, that Albert did indeed have them in his possession, and that there had indeed been reasonable cause for the authorities to enter the warehouse.

Albert said, "Yes, indeed." Then he clobbered Ron Cloud in court with a briefcase full of slick side-steps. The mobiles had been already out of their cartons and on the shelves when they were confiscated. No labels, no cartons or invoice numbers. Albert had bought himself time to do this by noticing that the first warrant used for the search had the numbers in his address reversed. Albert produced bills of sale for "one lot of plasticware, paid in full, to Albert J. Niklozak," which *could* have referred to the mobiles. Albert also had a cancelled check that might have been used to purchase the mobiles. Oddly, the check had been made out to one "Buster Cook," who had been dead for years, but Ron Cloud didn't know that.

Albert's performance on the stand was John Garfield perfect, ending with his turning to the jury and telling them, "Ladies and gentlemen, I apologize for this terrible larry of a mess—which has so wasted your valuable time here today."

Ron Cloud Carlini sat seething; he was lucky to get out of court with his license to practice still intact. Albert was so happy after the verdict was announced that he gave his lawyer a trip to Las Vegas, along with $1,000 worth of quarters.

He sent Ron Cloud a roll of nickels and one of the plastic baby mobiles, gift wrapped.

Albert kept rolled coins in his desk and always carried three separate stashes of money on the job. His show roll was a horse-choking wad of fives and tens that he'd peel through for effect. His real money was around his neck in a leather sack. And his girl-money he kept stuffed in his shirt pocket, right above his heart.

Even though Albert's mind and wallet were caught up with the warehouse, his heart belonged to his string of working girls.

By all accounts they idolized Albert and would work for no one else. He spoiled them, he cajoled them, he worked out their Ann Landers problems for them; he tried to keep the drugs and the sauce from completely ruining their looks and their lives.

He felt that, as a graduate of the Roman Catholic school system, he was required to keep his prostitutes healthy and clean, free from disease, from melancholy, and from moral turpitude.

Sometimes, his inbred disposition toward bare-knuck-led fighting got the better of him and he'd raise a hand to one of the girls. I once had to help bail him out of jail for punching an old-timer. As I drove him home, his shirt was stained with blood and whiskey, his eyes clouded with beer and shame.

On the strength of the money generated by his ware-house and his working girls, but mostly due to his morality and his efficiency, Albert was becoming the guy whom people around the neighborhood went to for things. Here was a guy that we had all known since Saint Mary's, who held a bit of the romance and unspoken power of the Yacovazzi Brothers, but with none of the fear that the split-nose crowd generated. Albert was a guy still in his twenties who could reach into his pocket or his bag of tricks or his Rolodex, and solve a problem for you—without making you feel shitty for asking.

I went to him myself a couple times. When Annetta got pregnant, there were complications with the pregnancy. I was making nine grand a year from the school district and I had a deductible on our medical coverage even for child-birth. I forget how much the deductible was, but we didn't have it. I had visions of the establishment holding onto my wife and my son there in the hospital as collateral, until I came up with the money.

Albert was my plug-angel, and he supplied the money I

needed—no questions, no condescension, no vigorish. Annetta and I agreed that Albert would be the boy's *Compare*.

We would have done that anyway.

When James Albert was not yet a year old and needed some minor surgery, I went to Albert again. He didn't even get off the phone as he peeled me the bills and then waved his hand at my thanks— "Forget about it."

After Arlynn Svenson had invited me into the upstairs girls bathroom, I told Albert about her. He warned me off that and reminded me that pussy-pursuit had led to the downfall of more men than money-hunting and power-grabbing put together. Ted Kennedy had already driven off the Chappaquiddick bridge by then. Albert recapped the story of John Profumo and Christine Keeler for me, and pointed out that this high school muff of mine could not be nearly as sweet as was Keeler, and I was nowhere near as secure in my job as had been Profumo.

I told Albert that I appreciated the input. Then he had told me about "taking care of things" before a woman could mess you up.

Yes, Albert was the local wishing well all right, an option to be considered, used, and appreciated—but not to be taken advantage of.

But as things turned out, I went to that wishing well one too many times in my life.

❖

January 8, 1971, in a bar:

"Bugs Bunny."

"Nah, Steve McQueen. Albert, we're never gonna agree here."

"On this?"

"On this, on anything. We'll never agree."

"Probably not. You're probably right. But, you have to see it that Bugs is cool. You're perfectly right, though. We will never agree."

"Maybe it's because that our criteria is so different, right? Our standards of judgment. You know, Steve and Bugs, they probably wouldn't even get nominated up against each other. They'd be in different categories."

"Maybe."

"Albert, see, McQueen, see, I remember him as Josh Randall for example. One time, he's coming down this hall-way, in this rooming house—that's what they always called them, rooming house. So this guy jumps out, clobbers him with a shotgun butt, the wooden handle, right to the side of the head. That's the first time I realized what it was to be really hurt like that, what it felt like. YOU probably know, but I don't know. See, I looked at him on the television, I said, 'Oh, I see.' It burns. Albert, it burns. Taking a shot, from a heavy, slamming wooden object, that's how it feels."

"Wood's bad, but nothing's worse than metal. I'd rather take it to the head with wood than with metal, anytime."

"Guy can act though. Guy's okay."

"You know who's cool too? All those old guys in the movies, they wear gray suits and hang around sucking mar-tinis. Or else they're sitting in a nightclub in a tuxedo, sit-ting at a table with some broad with blond kinky hair, then Slapsy Maxie Rosenbloom comes over and sits down with them for awhile. You know the kind of guy I mean, I'm talking about? I can't think of their names."

"Like Adolph Menjou, old guys like that?"

"Yes, exactly. Tasti, you always know what I'm talking about. Adolph Menjou, guys like that. Very cool in their own way."

"Those guys back then, even if they were only going out to rob a liquor store, they'd always wear a suit and tie."

"And a hat."

"Oh yeah, they are all very cool. Guys like Regis Toomey."

"Yeah. And, uh, Francois Tone."

"No, I think it's FRANCHOT Tone."

"Franchot? Franchot's not a name, is it? I'm from Europe and it's not even a name over there. Franchot's no name."

"No, it's not, but for him it is."

"Yeah but, yeah. But Bugs, man, the man can do it all. Everything they ask of him. Boy can act, the boy can sing a song, dance, tell jokes. The rest of these cartoon guys, they can't even get close. Somebody like Mickey Mouse? Tasti, it's not even close. Mouse is gonna deliver a joke? You ever watch him? You get your eyes off the famous Funicello lumps for a second, you watch the mouse try to tell a joke? It's painful, baby, to watch and to see it. Let Bugs do it."

"No, you're absolutely right, the mouse, severely overrated, got more history than texture to him, but still, I'm trying to explain about McQueen here."

"Wait. Bugs is so good, they actually duplicated him. They duplicated him, they got Daffy Duck. Who you think Daffy Duck is, with just a different voice? He's Bugs, man. He's Bugs. Same guy. Same wise-ass personality. Let me tell you, all the great ones, Tasti, they change the way the game is played by everyone who comes after them. They get their shoulders all bloodied from everyone else standing on them from then on. That bunny has bloodied his shoulders with the weight of those who came after him. To reach further and higher. That's Bugs. That's what he did."

"Albert, I'm thinking you enjoy him so much cause you're just like him. You got that goofy personality, that outlaw outlook. You see yourself in him."

"Nah, he's not. He's like anyone, he's like YOU, for God's sake. You're goofy, funny character, you're singing all the time. Bugs ain't like me. He's like anyone, he's like YOU. Now, if I'M like anyone, I'm like your man there— McQueen. See, I got the cool. I got the cold-blooded smile. I even ride motorcycles. I'm so fearless, don't give a shit. Not too tall. I'm like your man there. McQueen."

"You?"

"Yeah."

"McQueen?"

"Yeah. And you're Bugs."

"So, Albert, now wait a minute. What we've just said here, this—we both of us chose guys that remind us of each other. Not of ourselves, but of each other?"

"Yeah, God, you're right. It's sickening to say that and think it. God."

"Yeah, it certainly is. Let's not even think about it. Please."

SIX

BOTH OF US needed reinforcement at the end of our work-weeks, and so on some Fridays Albert and I would meet up for a bar run. He'd need to forget about all the scams he'd been dealing with for five days; I'd need to forget some of the ugly school scenes, and the bad decisions, and the pent-up/cooped-in boredom, and the truckload after truckload of troubled kids. Kids like Arlynn Svenson.

Young teachers have the burden of remembering how hard it is just to survive the experience of high school.

I had run the four-forty in track—four years of bearing left.

In early June of Arlynn's senior year, we senior advisors took her and about seventy other near-graduates on a class trip to Jones Beach. By four o'clock of that long afternoon, the heat and the din of teenagers was grinding on me and I had to get away for awhile. I told another advisor that I was going to patrol the dunes for beer drinkers and couples making out. I started walking down West End Beach, past the green flag, then the yellow, then the red. This was West End One, not West End Two. A seaplane flew by tugging a banner about Bosco, so rich and chocolate-y.

About half a mile down the beach, I stopped and looked out at the waves, and then headed up into the dunes, where I laid out a blanket and collapsed for awhile by myself. The sound of the waves breaking cut across the top of the dunes. Even with my eyes closed to the sun, I could sense the red-slatted hurricane fence curling down the beach through the dunes behind me. It had been blown down flat every few yards but then twisted back upright. Sharp, three-foot-high blades of weed sprang up from the sands through the slats in the fence. I felt surrounded, and protected.

As I rolled over on the blanket, I could feel the heat on

my arms and chest, the little puddle of sweat clinging above my stomach, and the sand in my bathing suit.

I was almost asleep when I heard a thin voice calling out my name. I looked up to see Arlynn Svenson tiptoeing over the sand dune toward me. She kept squealing, "Ow, it's hot," until she made it to my blanket and stood there on one of its corners. She began walking in place, lifting her feet a bit. "Ooch," she said, "Ooch, ooch, it hurts, that feels good." Her steps were leaving little chunks of sand on the blanket.

I propped myself up on an elbow and held my hand out in front of my eyes. Arlynn was wearing a black one-piece bathing suit. She had a gold chain with a tiny "A" around her left ankle. She smiled and waved twice and she crashed down onto her knees on the blanket a few inches from me. She grinned and rocked a bit and said to me, "Wow, huh?"

I looked around the dunes and tried to use my teacher voice as I said, "So the sand's hot, huh?"

She smiled some more. Waved at me again, using a little kid's hand motion—open and close, open and close. Then she seemed to remember that she was upset with me, and she gave me her afternoon-television pout. "You haven't been in your room after school," she told me. "I been coming for you."

I told her I'd been busy, with June and graduation and all. I was trying not to look at her.

"Hey, don't call me my name, okay?" She leaned in. "Jay," she said to me, "Jay, I like how you lips go when you call me Coochie. Call me that instead."

I readjusted myself on my elbow and I asked her how she was enjoying the trip.

She said, "Oh, okay, I guess. Okay, but I get a little bored. You know me. Always something."

"Yeah," I told her, "Yeah, well."

She leaned her head a bit down closer toward me. "How about you? I bet you get bored too sometimes, don't you?"

"Sometimes, I guess so," I told her. "Not much."

She waited awhile. I still held out the dumb hope that if I didn't say anything she would go away, although this technique had never worked with Arlynn as long as I'd known her.

She straightened herself up a bit, looked around, waited a beat, and said to me, "The sand looks so pretty. I love it here." She moved her hand and her eyes across the sightline of the dunes. "I guess we're both sort of alone up here, huh. All by ourself."

I said, "Well."

My only hope was to give her nothing to key off. Maybe she'd leave. Maybe.

I had once seen Arlynn drive herself into a violent rage that I suspected was for real. It happened outside the main office as the principal was trying to get her to go home. First she stood making some rhythmic little noises without opening her mouth. Then she began twisting her head around to strange angles as she yelled out curses. She took a kick at the filing cabinets. As the principal grabbed and held her arm, Arlynn fell limp, dangling. He lowered her down onto the floor. When she looked up and saw me watching, she dropped her head down and cried. Her fingers were scratching at the dirty linoleum floor.

In the dunes now, I said to her, "Arlynn, we'd better get back to everybody else. Okay? Okay, I'm going back now. C'mon."

I made a motion with my head as I felt the sun on my chest and the sand in my bathing suit grinding at my skin.

The top panel of her black bathing suit was held in place by two strings that were tied together behind her neck. She said to me, "Wait, before we go." Looking at me with eyes that were once the sole property of Lard the mystery man, she reached both hands back to the tie and she asked me casually, "Jay, do you want to look at myself for awhile?"

I shook my head, told her, "No. I better not."

Her fingers were working the strings behind her head as

she tipped her head left and right, like a doll. She said, "Come on. It's all right. I don't care. There's nobody here."

"Arlynn."

She got the strings untied and fairly slowly she brought the top of the bathing suit down. It folded over onto her lap. "See," she said, raising her voice to a baby-like pitch and tone, "They want to say hello to you. Jiggle, jiggle." She twisted her shoulders quickly back and forth to make the breasts flop a little. She was smiling at me. I was still propped on one elbow there on the beach blanket. I stayed still and I looked.

"Jiggle, jiggle."

Arlynn didn't take her eyes off me. She told me in that same voice, "They like you, Jay. Why don't you touch them a little bit? Do you want to?" She leaned closer to me.

Naturally, by then my bathing suit had become a tent big enough to hold Boy Scouts.

Years after I had left my family's house in Duck Alley, I had gone back to tour through the old place. Standing on the back porch, I saw the cigarette burns that my father's Chesterfields had made in the window sill as he would sit there, watching. Either a coffee cup or an ashtray, or maybe wine, had left a black circle in the wood.

I pictured my father trying to grab air for his lungs from the thick, wet atmosphere of the house.

Autistically, I reached out my hand toward Arlynn until my fingers came within an inch of the top of her breast. The hand stopped, the distance from God's fingers to man's, the little synapse of creation.

Arlynn called me a big silly and she told me, "Go ahead. Go touchie."

My fingertips grazed her skin, just a fraction of a world above her left areola. My hand drew back then, I shook my head, I looked down hard at the blanket I was lying on.

I didn't look up at her but I heard her ask me, "What else can we do now? Can we both do something else? So we don't get bored."

After he had switched to filtered cigarettes, my father would smoke the butts down until the last drag burned black into the fiber of the filter.

Arlynn asked me, "What else can we do now? Can we both do something else? So we don't get bored."

On our ride home from the hospital with our newborn child, Annetta had me drive five miles out of our way to avoid going over railroad tracks. We had an old Volkswagen bus with terrible suspension, and she was still in hemorrhoidal pain from the delivery.

Arlynn was asking me, "What else can we do now? Can we both do something else? So we don't get bored."

I had walked the streets of Mineola with my heels barely touching pavement after Dr. Thomas Malifollo had woken me in the hospital lobby and told me that I was a father.

"What else can we do now?" she was asking me.

There are two stories to tell you about what happened next there on the beach—there's the fantasy and the real.

First, the fantasy—and I have to point out that it's been a very useful myth for me, to be used in times of need for years after that moment, used in social-erotic situations of both twos and ones.

In this version, I stretch myself up toward Arlynn's face and I say, "Well, I don't know what we can do. What else do you have, Arlynn, that I can get to know about you, to keep us from getting bored?"

And she rocks forward up onto her knees then, and gently, so smoothly, curls the bottom of her bathing suit down over her ass onto her thighs, showing me that little black spot of hair, and I rise up to take her shoulders then, and she rolls back onto the plaid wool blanket, me so gently on top of her, as very quickly my knees and her heels start digging deep and perfectly round imprints into the sand there beneath the blanket.

Or sometimes everything's flipped around, with her riding on top of me.

At first I try to keep our lust-dance in rhythm with the hard pounding of the Atlantic, the sound that she and I can hear breaking and receding like a drum just over the wind-raked dunes. We are aware of our own noises and of the weight of the water cracking down into the moist sand and then lapping back out to sea—smooth and free.

But keeping that nature-beat is impossible for me, and so she and I begin moving faster and harder. Sometimes it seems as if the ocean would pick up *its* beat, trying to get in tandem with us, faster and harder, as I move myself into this perfumed receptacle, me driving mine into her eager place . . . into . . . into . . .

Okay, now here's the real . . .

As I drew my hand back away from her during that moment in the dunes, after looking at her breasts, I tried to form some thoughts for awhile, and the only thought I could come up with was this: Here in front of me is a pair of virginal seventeen-year-old breasts, and they are nowhere near as lovely or inviting as those of my wife at home. Breasts that have been suckled by our son for months now, and are much smaller than these I see before me, and yet, they are breasts which I want to touch so much more than I want these.

And since I'm telling the truth here, I may as well tell it all—the top of each of Arlynn's breasts was covered by teenage acne. They were big enough to sag a bit, even at her age, and they were a dull white color there underneath the white Jones Beach sun, and they were much too bright and real and too dull to be inviting, except for the allure of the debauchery value that they had attached to them.

And so I did the right thing that afternoon. Maybe not for all the right reasons, but I did the right thing.

Although I didn't do it the right way. What I tried to say to Arlynn then was, "Arlynn, we can't. I am your teacher. I am married. I am a father."

But that nice, smooth, short paragraph of dialogue somehow got truncated by the raging blood that was getting pumped into my ears and other extremities. And so instead of— "Arlynn, we can't. I am your teacher. I am married. I am a father," the words came out: "Arlynn, we can't. I am your father."

Arlynn looked at me for awhile, probably thinking she had finally entered the world of her soap operas for real.

After a moment she just said, "Oh, okay," as if she were accepting my word for her heritage, and we went back down the beach toward the bus, walking apart.

Most of what the nuns had tried to teach us in grammar school I had disregarded over the years. Their foolish list of patron saints—one for everything in the world from lost causes to dish towels—seemed so formal and methodic for the spiritual world.

Yet, some of what the nuns taught me has stayed within the make-up of my psyche for a lifetime. For one thing, I pray. I don't go to church, I don't trust God, I don't know where my last pair of rosary beads finally wound up, but I do pray. Every morning and every night. Almost all of the stuffing has gone out of the words by now—it's like cheering for the Knicks after the game has been lost. Still, at least the words are still there, in my head. Maybe they're not really prayers but just a chant—something to rake out my head so that I can get to sleep or get myself out of bed in the morning. I still call them my prayers.

And, every morning and night of my life, I end those prayers with a thank-you to God for that moment in the dunes of Jones Beach with Arlynn Svenson. A thank-you for how that one scene turned out.

Because, if I had gone the other way, if I had said to her, "What else can you show me, Arlynn, to keep us from getting bored?", then even if the tragedy that was to come to all of us would have been no more tragic, my hand in it would have been heightened.

My innocence on the beach has been a thin but vital oxygen line for me through the years.

And so every night I go to bed with these words: "And thank you, dear God, for putting pimples on the breasts of Arlynn Svenson."

❖

January 15, 1971, at the kitchen table:

"*I'm just saying, sometimes some people, even the married ones, they try to communicate, they don't always know how.*"

"*How?*"

"*How? Okay, I'll give you a how. One day I was out working, see? And Annetta, she's home, she finds this grasshopper sitting in the middle of the bathroom floor. Peaceful. He sitting there, he's not hurting anybody, he's a grasshopper. Now Annetta's no biologist, but still, anyone who's lived on Long Island should recognize a grasshopper when you see one, right? Instead, she—because she lived her early years in some dark little corner of Jamaica somewhere—my wife looks at this little hopper and what she sees instead—a cockroach.*"

"*Oh, yeah?*"

"*Yeah, that's what she thinks. So the bug's waiting patiently to be shown the way out. You know, he's just a grasshopper, he's saying, 'Excuse me, I wandered in here. I'll be on my way now.' But instead, Annetta's there, she's panicking. Cockroach. She's all of a sudden making these clumsy attempts to step on the thing. But he's juking her pretty good, left and right, left and right. This guy's Hugh McElhenny. He's Crazy Legs Hurst all of a sudden, for crying out loud. So she leaves the bathroom, leaves the grasshopper alone with his thoughts for a few minutes, but then she comes back in, see? And now, she's packing aerosol.*"

"*Black Flag?*"

"*I think so.*"

"*That's the best there is. We use it in the warehouse.*"

"*She's got both eyes on the bug, both her thumbs are on*

the red button, and the little guy's eyes are following her around in a circle. Just following her around."

"So what?"

"So here's the part about communication. This measly little grasshopper, he begins exhibiting an intelligence far beyond his normal phylum. He apparently tries to communicate with this dangerous woman in the only way it knows how. You know how?"

"How?"

"He starts hopping."

"How you know all this?"

"She told me. I figured it out later. So anyway, it's hopping, it's hopping, again and again, high and proud, it's proclaiming, 'Look at me, woman! Could a cockroach do THIS?' It's hopping proud."

"Sit down, Tasti, you'll spill everything, I know what a hop looks like, for Christ sake. Just tell the story. You're so bad at telling stories."

"So Annetta she interprets this hopping as an attack. 'My God, this cockroach is attacking me. Might be rabid.' She screams out, she closes her eyes, she plunges the button, both her thumb nails are turning white with the pressure."

"Wow. Some story. Is there anything to eat?"

"The deadly mist, it engulfs the innocent victim, it positively saturates its little lungs. It continues to hop, the only thing it knows to do, each little hop announcing still, 'I am u grasshopper . . . I hop grass . . . I am a hopper of the grass.' But I have to tell you, Albert, by now every little hop is gaining less and less altitude. Its last little hop barely gets his feet off the tile floor there."

"This is so sad. I feel like Marlin Perkins now."

"Yeah. When I got home, I swaddled the little body up in toilet paper, paid proper respects, I flushed it away to the ages."

"Why you telling me this?"

"I give you this story to show you this point. Many

intelligent people often point out this—that lack of commu-
nication is the root problem of our society."

"Yeah, but nobody ever listens to them."
"You know what I mean?"
"What?
"You know what I mean?"
"Huh?"

SEVEN

ONLY TWO WEEKS were left in the school year, and in Arlynn's educational career, after our near-tryst in the sand dunes of West End Beach. Whenever I saw her around school she seemed suddenly distant now—quiet and vague—as if she were trying to do everything the direct opposite of her normal style. What she was actually doing was giving me signs as to what was to come, but I didn't pick up on any of it. Looking back, I can see that it was nothing more than your normal descent into melancholia and madness.

Arlynn was used to showing up for school dressed in one of her "Hey, look what I got in here" sweaters, pulled down over a coordinated skirt that was shorter than a freshman composition. Her everyday make-up made her look like she had just gotten back from a slumber party with Lucille Ball and Bette Davis in *Baby Jane*.

But now she walked the halls with her face scrubbed bare and the rest of her appearance shooting for that frumpy/sack-cloth/beatnik look—loose sweatshirts, baggy Salvation Army pants, sneakers that were worn untied and didn't even bother to match each other.

She had a habit of holding the lower half of her left thumb up to her mouth and then sliding her lips across it like she was Paul Butterfield on a harmonica riff. That tick grew much worse now. It would come more often, more pronounced, almost violent, and she would show her teeth above the skin of the thumb. The base of her thumb stayed red and wet and swollen—constantly callused.

The expression on her face and the way she moved her legs and arms gave the impression that she wasn't heading from one place to another as much as she was simply drifting there.

When she spoke, it was with her head down and her voice low. She kept using my first name and I kept reminding her not to. Sometimes she would apologize. Sometime she would ignore me. Once she asked, "Why shouldn't I? After what we've been through, what we've been to each other, isn't that okay, to call your name?"

I told her no, it wasn't.

She said quietly, like to herself, "Jay, Jay, Jay, Jay, Jay."

Sometimes she would be singing something under her breath, and whenever I strained forward to listen, it was always the same song— "Kind of a Hush" by Herman's Hermits.

She asked me to proofread three letters for her before she sent them out. They were addressed to Derek, Frank and Barry. The letters spoke about past secret meetings and about that portion of her life being over now and about getting on with their lives. All the *i*'s in the three letters were dotted with little hearts.

I debated showing the letters to somebody, but they really didn't say much. No words of self-destruction, just what sounded like midnight ramblings of a strange little mind. When she came to pick the letters up from me, I asked her who these three guys were. They were Herman's Hermits, the guitar players and drummer.

I said to her, "Arlynn, I was wondering how you've been feeling lately. I've been concerned."

"I feel no good. You know that."

"I wonder, I was wondering if you should go see somebody about it maybe."

"You mean a doctor?"

"Yes, maybe somebody like that. Somebody who could help out."

"I already did."

"Oh, you have? You've seen someone?"

"Yes, sure I have. I seen a doctor, to help."

"You sure? Do you mean for real? You went to see somebody? Tell me the truth now, Arlynn."

"Of course. Of course for real. And I'm getting him to help."

"That's good. That's very good, I think. And that's very important for you."

"Thank you for asking about me. Jay, I think you really do care about me sometimes, don't you?"

I came back to my classroom from lunch the next day to find a corked vile of yellow liquid waiting for me on my desk. I assumed that the stuff was urine—this was a public high school, after all—and a quick sniff proved me correct. I slid the stuff into my desk drawer for the warm afternoon. At three o'clock, I slipped the vile into my palm, emptied it into the faculty room men's toilet, and tossed the glass into a dumpster on my way out of the building.

I went straight home and tried to forget about the day and about this troubled girl.

Both my wife and I had accepted the fact that our marriage was a strange one. We should have both been forewarned; even my marriage proposal had gone against the grain of romantic tradition.

While awaiting my ring-bearing arrival, Annetta had put a pot of tea on the hot plate in her room and she had somehow spilled the boiling water, badly scolding both of her arms. The attendant at the emergency room wrapped her arms and hands in gauze and cotton, leaving the ring finger of the left hand free, at the insistence of the burn victim.

She took on the look of Boris Karloff in *The Mummy* giving a vaguely crude gesture with his left hand.

I proposed and she accepted, but I could only get the ring as far as the knuckle of her red and blistered finger. As we embraced, she had to slip the white unbending pegs that were her arms underneath the arm pits of my gray windbreaker. It occurred to me that her arms must be looking like elephant tusks.

Arlynn called me at home. It was the first time she had done that, and it discomforted me. It seemed to me that she had broken down a barrier that I badly needed. She said that she had to talk to me. I told her that it would have to be in school the next day.

She said, "It can't wait. Jay? Now, please."

I told her no, that I was sorry, and I hung up.

Annetta tried to read my face, asked me who it was.

I said, "Just some student asking for homework. I hate it when they call me here like that."

She nodded. She went in to feed James Albert.

Annetta and I had enjoyed a honeymoon, but not an actual honeymoon-period in our marriage. Just the opposite. It wasn't until the supposed grace tenure was over that we really started accepting our union. It had taken almost a year for us to manage to become more comfortable with each other full-time, and more willing to hammer the outlines of our previous lives alone into a unified form that was more conducive to our living as one.

The time after the birth of our son saw us both become more committed to being pliant for each other and being a bit more selfless.

Annetta and I needed a new apartment so that the baby could have his own room. We had both decided that she would not work until our kid was in school, so we could only afford a crumby little apartment that was the second floor of a crumby little house in a worse section of Manorhaven than our last place. I was still paying off college loans.

The owners of the place lived below us. Annetta had resented the apartment ever since the moment I had tried to carry both her and our son over its threshold and realized that I wasn't going to make it. I had to, like King Solomon, chose between the two. Instead of making a decision, I hesitated and then dropped Annetta on the floor.

I think her resentment of the place was mixed with some guilt over not being a working mother. "I don't know what it is I want sometimes, Jay," she said to me. "I want to be James Albert's mother, but I want to make other things happen for us too. Do you know what I mean?"

"Do you know what I mean?" I asked Arlynn the day after her phone call. She had caught up with me in the parking lot. I had my car key in my hand. I took a step toward her and I asked her again, "Do you understand?"

"What do you mean?"

"Arlynn, I'm worried about you, we all are. Let me talk to Guidance about you, for you. I just don't want to come in here one day and find out, well, find out something bad. I don't know."

"Bad?"

"Yeah, has happened to you."

"Something bad has happened to me?"

"That's right. I just don't want that to happen."

"It already happened, didn't it? But it's all right, Jay. It's the beginning of something, not the end. I told you I was taking care of it, and taking good care of myself. Don't worry."

"What?"

"Of us. I think, as people grow up, they have to start looking at things different, don't you? That they can't just be silly and thinking about themselves the whole time."

"No, that's true. That's a very mature way to look at things. You have to start being an adult."

"Right. Adult. Now, in the situation I'm in, I have to start thinking about more than just me, don't I? It's *us*, now too, isn't it? You too."

"What?"

"I told you I was taking care of things for us. Didn't you get my sample? You got it."

"Your what?"

"My sample I left you. The rabbit. He's dead, Jay. Isn't that sort of great? In a way though?"

"Arlynn."

"Isn't that a funny way to say it though? You've heard that, right? That the rabbit died? They don't really use a rabbit, do they?"

"Arlynn."

"It's okay. It's all right. Jay, honey, I haven't told a soul. Not a soul even. There's no one to tell even if I wanted to, baby. But still, now we have to talk, don't we?"

"What about?"

"Shhh, baby, shhhh." Arlynn stepped forward and she tried to put her finger on my lips. I flinched.

"Jay, don't talk. We have some decisions to make. Both of us. I want both of us in on whatever we decide to do. Don't you think? Don't you think that's right?"

"Arlynn."

She reached out to my lips again. I swatted her hand away.

"Jay. Please. Jay, don't walk away. Jay. Don't walk away from me now. Please, honey, I need you. We need each other. Get out of the car. Get out of the car. Jay. Please. Right *now*."

❖

December 15, 1971, at the undertakers:

"Jeez, Tasti, I'm really sorry, I don't know what to say. Which is so much unlike me."

"Yeah, thank you, Albert."

"He was a good guy, for such an old guy, huh?"

"Oh, yeah."

"Oh, sure. You can tell me about it, if you want to. I don't know."

"Nah, that's okay."

"Okay, that's fine too."

"Just . . ."

"Huh?"

"No, it's just, jeez, Albert, I didn't even know what this guy's life had been like, you know?"

"Oh, yeah? Like what?"

"Yeah, I thought that he just sat in front of the porch window for eighty years, you know? Just looking out at his lawn for his whole life. Staring straight. Not moving around or anything."

"Well, he was the Buddha of the Back Porch all right, right?"

"Yeah, he was. Still though, it turns out the guy was something when he was young. I mean, turns out he had adventures a guy like me could never dream about. And I never knew this. My compare got drunk at a wedding, he told me about it. I mean, my father had been a waiter in a speakeasy, in the city, in the twenties. He even served Al Capone once, when Big Al was back east."

"Oh, yeah? Capone? So your old man met him, huh? That's pretty good."

"And he got arrested in a raid at the gin mill this one

time. Maybe a couple times. He also got arrested back in Italy, trying to unionize the docks in Genoa. The dock workers. Ship builders. Got his head split open by the goons for trying to do that."

"Sounds like my kind of guy. Walked out there along the edge. Who would ever known."

"Yeah, it's sort of hard to believe, isn't it? I always knew he'd been a wetback here, but I never got a chance to know that other stuff about him. Now he's dead. And I never got to tell him."

"Tell him?"

"Tell him, yeah, I don't know, tell him that he was a somebody, y'know? And that I knew it. Not just some sad, foolish little guy sitting in the back porch window his whole life. Smoking a cigarette. I never got a chance to say to him, 'Hey, pop, now I know you were somebody. You lived your life. And I appreciate the value of that. I appreciate your life.' Never got a damn chance to tell him anything. Well, maybe I had the chance all right, just never used it."

"Yeah. There's a lot of things like that. That we never know until it's too late. A shitload of stuff we never get to say to people, I guess. I don't know."

"I should've been able to tell him. Should've made myself aware of it sooner. Should've asked around. Somebody would've told me. He himself was probably dying to tell me. But he was so quiet all the time. He figured, I guess, nobody asks, nobody cares, I ain't gonna bore my kid stiff with this stuff."

"Well, listen now, Tasti, you're telling ME now, right? It's not the same, but it's something, ain't it? Now there's one person who knows, at least. You keep telling people."

"My last time seeing him, in the hospital, he's lying there, two-three days worth of beard stubble on his face. I mean, other than that, he looked like crap too, but that was the thing that stuck with me. He was always such a dapper little guy. Always kept himself looking good. Always clean shaved, everyday. Even his day off. But you get him in that

93

stinking hospital bed, they figure, what the hell. He's too weak to do anything for himself, so the nurses they all figure, what the hell, he's dying anyway, let the old fart go to shit. He's lying there, he knows how he looks. He asked me to ask them. To shave him, you know? I told some nurse up there, but they never did. Maybe I should've done it myself. The one guy who finally DID get to shave him was Lavigne, I guess, the undertaker. The man should not have died feeling like he was some shit-bum."

"Those bastards."

"Yeah, well, no, it's all right though, cause you know what? I use that for my crying trigger. I'm not embarrassed to say this. The first day or so, I couldn't get any tears up. Until I thought about him dying like a three-day shit-bum, grubby beard, there in the hospital. Now I use it all the time. To kick-start things inside of me. To get me crying a little bit for him. Like now."

"Yeah, Tasti, you got me too now, doing it. Thanks a lot."

EIGHT

ACROSS THE TOPS of the houses and the dried lawns of the back yards, the sound of rubber hitting wood fanned out across the neighborhood. If you leaned your head out far enough through the window, you might be able to see the pink flight of the ball moving through air, then slamming the shingles, then bouncing back. Second hop, into the glove, starts again.

A gray sway-backed garage had come to us as part of the rent on our apartment. I would take a Pennsy Pinkie out to the alley each afternoon after teaching school, just to peg that ball against the broad side of the garage with its peeling paint and the chipped wood slats.

I liked to think that my delivery looked pretty good out there, even though I still was wearing my school shoes. Right-handed, but with that big kick and rocking motion that lefties favor—Spahn and Koufax. Like Albert with a chicken bone, up in the balcony.

First off I'd lean in and stare at the wall, getting the sign. Then I'd rock back, the big left wing-tip shoe reaching up and out, and the right arm in the Van Heusen white shirt would whip the rubber ball into the wall with an echo worthy of a catcher's mitt. My pants would be spotted with chalk dust from the classroom instead of with rosin. Close enough.

I even wore my mitt sometimes, one of those old, tiny, floppy, blackened-leather fielder's-gloves. I'd found it one June in a locker after the kids had cleared out for the year.

I pitched and I thought, sometimes keeping the count, sometimes setting up game situations in my head. Other times I thought about stuff other than baseball. Mostly I tried not to think about this thing with Arlynn Svenson.

Some pitches would be delivered in fury, and you could

hear my grunt on the follow-through, as if I could pack all of the problems and evil passions of my life into that old pink rubber ball, to be smashed and obliterated against the gray shingles.

Other times, I'd be out there throwing jazz-musician sad, moving slow, like I was hardly able to bend over to catch the ball on the second bounce as it came back off the wall. It was as if I didn't really want to be out there throwing, that I'd rather get on with other jobs—grading papers or setting the table or helping feed and change James Albert. But I had this job to do first.

I showed pretty good control. You could tell by the spot there, blackened by hours of afternoons—being smacked by the ball. The black splotch was bigger than a strike zone, but not by much, and you can tell that I knew to throw more low than high, working the inside corner, which is a good idea for any pitcher.

Sometimes I would make up stories so that I wouldn't have to think about what I didn't want to think about. Sometimes I was a hot-shot high school hurler, before the war, a Long Island kid with a shot at the big time. But the war interrupts, and afterwards, even though I signed a contract with Cleveland, I never got above double A ball, and when my father got sick, I had to get back to help run the business—dry goods—that I was destined to inherit.

Sometimes it was an injury that kept me from getting my shot. I was diving off a fifteen foot rock into Long Island Sound when I forgot to keep my arms tight by my sides and the force of hitting the flat top of the water ripped my shoulder apart for good.

Or maybe I just wasn't good enough for the Majors.

Whatever the reason, in this dream I never got over thinking about it, and I would take a trip back each afternoon for twenty minutes or so, before going in for supper.

I'd also remember real stories as I was out there, stories that maybe didn't mean much. Think about anything, just so I wouldn't be thinking about this thing with Arlynn Svenson.

When my godfather's only daughter had gotten married, I drove way out on the Island for the wedding. It had been a great Italian affair, lots of pasta and pork, dancing and drinking. My father was already pretty sick by then.

After most of the guests had left the hall, my *compare* and I had sat and nibbled breadsticks over a wine-splattered white tablecloth. There were just a few plates left that the waiters hadn't cleared yet; some of the plates had half-eaten pieces of wedding cake on them.

My *compare* seemed a little sad, and I told him a couple times what a great wedding he had thrown.

He said, "You know, she's been out of the house for four years now, so it shouldn't be a big thing her getting married. Still though. Still there's a little bit of me feels bad though."

"Well, kids grow up," I told him, as if that explained it.

"Yeah, I guess so. But her mother's off in Canada somewhere, couldn't even get back for this. What's with that?"

"Yeah. Yeah."

"I'm reminding you now about you mother. I'm sorry. I didn't think."

"That's okay."

"This whole thing here cost me five grand, did you know that? I'm gonna have to borrow to cover everything."

"It's a day she'll never forget," I told him.

"Yeah, but I got no wife. I got no money. Now I got no daughter. My son he's flying out. So what's left?"

I looked around, uncomfortable.

He asked me again, "Jay, what's left for me now?"

"Well," I told him, "You still got some of this cake." And I gave him my best stupid grin.

After a moment he started grinning too, and he said to me, "Well, that's right, *ghumba*, I got some cake at least."

He laughed some and then he picked up a piece of the

cake and tried to slide it into the side pocket of his tuxedo jacket, smearing the white icing along the black material. He said, "I save some of it."

That started me laughing into tears, and I couldn't talk clearly, I just pointed at the mess he was making. "It's no real pocket there, *Compare*," I tried to tell him, "it's just a sewed-on."

He just shrugged and laughed some more. He told me it was rented anyhow.

It was probably a bad idea to meet Arlynn Svenson alone again, but I felt that I had to talk to her and I couldn't think of anyone in the world that I would want to be there with us, listening.

I asked her to drop by my classroom after school, when everyone had gone home except for detainees, janitors, and maybe the principal. She smiled and said, "Certainly, Mr. Tasti," as if I had been setting up these after-hours meetings with her for years. She was there at 3:10, wearing a black, hooded sweatshirt and gray sweatpants.

"What happened to the side of your face?"

She reached up to run her thumb lightly across the blue and red welt that was spread from the outer half of her right eye back into her hair.

She told me, "Nothing, I don't know, I must've fell into something." Making sure I knew that she was lying. Her eyes—probably yearning for the mascara that had been their constant companion for at least seven years—were blood-veined, a bit swollen, looking ready to tear.

During my first year of teaching, one student who would sit alone in the back of the room asked to go to the nurse three days in a row, because of a cut on his hand. Each day his palm would be bleeding with a bit of flesh pulled back open. I kept asking him what had happened, he kept shrugging me off. Finally, I checked his desk and found a jagged kink of metal where part of the book-holder had been twisted off. I carried the desk down to the janitors closet and I vowed to make my classes less noxious.

"No, nothing." Arlynn shook her head. "I must've just fell into something."

I was sitting watching her from behind my desk, its top fortified from her with piles of ungraded papers, notebooks, yellow attendance cards, a gray stapler, a desk calendar, *The Great Gatsby*, a baseball sitting in a tiny inverted plastic Mets cap, a small picture of Emily Dickinson taped onto a box holding memo cards, a plaster form of all of the teeth in my head, and a mug that said, "Sick, sick, sick," on its side and was holding pencil stubs, nearly drained ballpoints, paper clips and a spoon.

I pointed over at one of the metal-and-green plastic student desks and I said to her, "Arlynn, sit down. Please. We have to start talking to each other here."

She didn't move. "What's there to talk about?"

"Arlynn, I don't think that either one of us has an idea even of what's going on."

"Yeah, we do. We both know. Maybe we just don't like it, so we try to get it to be all confusing and everything. But it's not confusing at all. The both of us made a mistake. It don't matter. The world don't care about us and our mistakes, Jay. We're just like little buckets in the water, that's all."

"Please, Arlynn, you have to start calling me Mr. Tasti again. I've told you that. I'm not Jay."

"Yes, you are. You were Jay before, right?"

"What? When was I ever Jay?"

She smiled at me. "Okay, doesn't matter."

"Okay. It matters. Anyway, you don't want to sit while we talk? Sit down? No? You sure? Okay, then, please, Arlynn, just listen and stay with me, please. Can you do that? Listen to what I'm saying to you? Right through to the end? Please?"

"About what? Us?"

"First, Arlynn, I have to ask about drugs and stuff. Or

too much drinking. I don't know, but I ask. It's the way you been acting."

"You don't have to worry about the baby, you know. I already took care of that little thing. All by myself."

"What? You what?"

"Oh, yeah. Everybody thinks I'm poor little Arlynn, that I can't do nothing for myself. Just poor little dumb Arlynn, that's all. All of you. My dumb father creep. Derek. Barry. Frank. Even Peter now. You. You too, Jay. They all of you think I can't do nothing by myself. Well, nobody got to worry about me. It's all over now. All gone."

"Arlynn. Arlynn, listen. There was no baby." I looked quick at the window of the closed classroom door. "Now was there, Arlynn? Or *was* there?"

"So now there's no baby, Jay? Is that what you're saying now? I got the doctor papers, Jay. I saved every single thing they give me. I got my test results from the rabbit, and, and the operation form I signed, and, and everything. You bastard."

I felt a tingling feeling crawling into my stomach and crotch. "Arlynn, I guess I don't know, maybe there was a baby, you say so. But why are you saying it to me, huh? You talk like it's mine. You must know what that could do, what that would mean. Haven't we been friends? Haven't we, huh?"

She didn't answer me.

"Arlynn. Listen. It is time to begin acting like an adult lady. In your life. Arlynn?"

"I'll think about it."

"Yes. And anyway, Arlynn, whatever it is that's happened to you here, you have to deal with the truth here. You have to know what is real and what is not, and you have to base all your actions upon that. Upon being an adult lady. Not on . . . not on some kind of television world you've managed to dream up for yourself to live in. You have to live in *this* world, Arlynn, it's the only one that's real. Please, Arlynn, listen to me. For the good of *you*. Please, girl. Listen to what is real and what is not."

She touched the bruise on her face and mumbled something.

"What'd you say?"

She rubbed her thumb violently back and forth across her teeth, then pulled her arm down, smacking it into her side. "You bastard. I tried to keep you quiet, your name. Now I'm gonna tell everybody there is about us. Everyone's gonna know everything there is about us. Everyone is gonna know how you been treating me."

"Arlynn. There's nothing to tell them. Nothing happened with us. Please."

She pulled the corners of her mouth down, she seemed to try to flush out a few tears. When none appeared, she hid her face with both her hands, fingers spread wide apart, and she turned and ran out of the room, banging a desk.

I had once sat in my classroom and watched through the window as two sophomores I knew were having a lovers' quarrel. The whole thing was played out for me in pantomime, out there on the lawn by the football field, with them thinking no one could see. The desperate looks, the dramatic turns of the body, the scene almost ended up with the back of a limp-wristed hand being held to a forehead, Sarah Bernhardt style.

All of these children were learning to deal with each other through watching the mannerisms and the surface realities of the no-life-span soap operas. Lousy shows with no touches of reality being shown on cloudy television screens in the middle of the boring afternoon. That was their truth.

In Arlynn's case, it was mannerisms and surface nonreality that completely engulfed her belief system. I could picture her running from our conversation, running all the way home, there to leap onto her bed and lie face down with angry feet and balled up little fists pounding at the bedspread. Then she would bury her head into the pillow and have a good cry. Christ Almighty.

Meanwhile, I sat there at my teaching desk and tried to figure out how to deal with things as they really were, and how they were really getting, for me.

To a young couple struggling to get used to the raising of a small child, there exists one entity which holds more power than drugs or guardian angels. It is a dependable baby-sitter. The right sitter can provide the power of escape better than any illegal dust, and she can supply more support than an angel.

Fortunately, Annetta and I had one, an Adelphi student who was also studying for her CPA. We used her one evening so that I could get Annetta away for a ride. We took 25-A all the way out to Cold Spring Harbor before swinging around back in and finally winding up right in Duck Alley.

There we got out of the car to walk awhile. The sun was red. I showed Annetta some of the old magical places—and I told her some of my stories. If she had heard them before, she didn't let me know. I showed her the statue of the Blessed Virgin, where we had given over our Mite Box money to the Niklozak family, to help them fight the Communists. I explained how, in a stick-ball game, if you hit the Virgin, it was a triple.

We wound up standing by the corpse of an old apple tree, out behind where Buster Cook's place used to be. I remembered how Cookie's old garage used to sit in one corner of the lot, barely holding onto an upright position. I even took a quick look around for Albert's cable-chain.

A patch of honeysuckle had spread from the cracks in the cement where the garage once stood. I went to it, picked one of its little yellow flowers, then bit off the tiny nipple and sucked out the bit of sweet. I showed Annetta how to do it; she had never heard of sucking the honey. A few buttercups were struggling in a corner of the concrete. I snapped off a couple of the little flowers and held them under Annetta's chin, checking the sun's reflection, showing her how to see if she liked butter.

With the honeysuckle and buttercups tossed to the ground, I looked around the overgrown lot we were standing in. I was surprised, maybe disappointed, at how little interest everything held for me.

Annetta and I had not reached that comfortable center in our marriage where I could sit and let my shoulders drop and tell her my troubles. As a first generation Italian-American, I still put too much weight on the first of those proper adjectives and too little on the second to feel right about whining to my wife. That's how I saw it. A part of me was—and always will be—my father. The man who silently took his problems with him out onto the back porch, there to sit with them as he gazed out the window at his back yard in America. The Buddha of the Back Porch.

I knew that when Arlynn started spreading her strange and ugly tale about us, that not only would my job be in danger, but my marriage and my family.

I had decided that one way to neutralize the effects, at least partially, would be to have the truth be known by as many people as possible, and as quickly as possible. But that had to start with a crowd of one. My wife.

That's what I had intended to do. That's why I had called upon the power of the baby-sitter for the evening. But I had been trying to share the truth with Annetta all the way out to Cold Spring Harbor and back. I couldn't find a way in.

We talked about our son, about the neighbors, about Duck Alley and the smell of dead wood. Everything except.

Then my wife told me, "Jay, I used to be afraid I'd be lonely my whole life. Now I'm afraid I'll just be helpless. I'll have to stand back and watch you suffer. And not be allowed to understand. And not be allowed to help. What is it that's going on, honey?"

So finally it was Annetta who opened the door for me.

She had been watching me struggle for days and now she let me know that. She asked me a question. Then she waited quietly for me to answer. She was doing what a loving wife did when concerned. She was doing exactly what I wanted her to do.

"Come on, Jay," she said. "I can only help you with it. I want to be allowed to do that."

I went over and sat on the tree stump, there in Buster Cook's back yard.

"Tell me, Jay."

I told her nothing.

Every teacher in my school knew the story of Paul Molicki.

Molicki had once been a Brooklyn-talking, back-slapping, shoulder-hugging English teacher who was a fierce advocate of the AFT, Albert Shanker's union that was trying to elbow out the less militant association as the sole bargaining agent for the teachers of the district.

Molicki's career as a union organizer and as an educator were snuffed out when he was accused of fondling two girls in his classroom after school.

Molicki maintained that the charges were trumped up by powers that didn't like his union militancy. He hinted at people on the school board, maybe even executives in the association. He fought the thing in the courts for over three years, using some of the lawyers and consultants that might have to help *me* if Arlynn spoke. Finally, Molicki wound up winning his suit, and he got a chunk of money in back pay for his years out of the classroom. He was reinstated at his old job.

But even in victory, his life had been wrecked. His marriage had oozed down into nothing, he was drinking, he was depressed. I was disheartened watching the effort it took for him to climb the steps into the school building each morning.

His eyes were glassy, worse after lunch, and he always had to wait a beat before responding to anything that you said to him. He was incapable of running a classroom, but the district knew that they couldn't fire him again. He was given the duty of permanent hall patrol. He walked the halls endlessly, moving like a zombie; even the kids got tired of mocking him.

He had gone from teaching *The Inferno* in his classroom to living it, out in the hall.

I didn't want to end up like him.

And so, with no idea of what else to do, or where else to go, I went to see my friend Albert Niklozak.

❖

January 15, 1971, in the Raspberry:

"Why did Johnny Fleischower get the shit kicked out of him by Sister Edelina that one time?"

"It wasn't Edelina, it was Teresa Marie. What time?"

"That worst time. His nose was bleeding so bad it was all over the floor, huh? All over his face, smeared up. His head got twisted around so that he was looking right at ME, for Christ sake. Like he didn't know what hit him. Looking at me with these two amazed eyes, like I was the one who done it."

"Yeah, well . . . he was on his knees, I remember, and she came over . . . "

"We were ALL of us on our knees, right? Weren't we? The whole class. Because we were praying from our knees, three o'clock, before we went home."

"Yeah, that's right. She was probably keeping us till five o'clock again, because she didn't like going back to the nun-house. Too hot back there."

"I remember we were saying the Apostles Creed."

"Yup. Yup. We were. 'I believe in God, the Father Almighty . . . '"

"And she stops us, remember? 'I believe in God, the Father Almighty, Creator of Heaven and Earth,' and she interrupts us, right? She asks us, real dramatic, 'Do you? Do you really?'"

"I guess we were taking it all too casual. And so Fleischower, he says to her . . . "

"He tells her, 'No, do you?' Great line. Amazing that he done it."

"So it went like this, 'I believe in God, the Father Almighty, Creator of Heaven and earth . . . '"

"'Do you? Do you really?'"

"'No, do you?'"

"Great . . . great . . . magnificent. Magnificat."

"And she comes up behind him, she hears him, so it's Pow— right in the kisser, Alice. Round house too, full force. Was it open-handed or fist?"

"I bet open-hand, but the heel of the hand, unsuspecting, clear shot, pop! All that nose bone twisted all the hell out of shape."

"What was that maniac Fleischower ever thinking? To come out and say that?"

"He should've been thinking, 'Great line I just got off, but I'm about to get my nose busted by a nun for it.'"

NINE

THE FAMILIAR LYSOL and cigar smell of the warehouse wasn't inviting or comforting for me this time in.

Albert was telling me, "Yeah, whatever you need, whatever it is, just get in line." He was kneeling on the floor, clipping labels, watching his own hands moving quickly, wildly, like trying to get rid of a swarm of gnats.

I just moved my lips a little to tell him yeah, I knew, I appreciated whatever he could do.

"Tasti, I can be a persuasive guy, if I have to be. You remember I followed Lou Cusack around for a whole afternoon stepping on the back of his shoes, huh?"

"Yeah, I remember that. He complained you broke both his feet. I don't remember what it was you wanted him to do though, that time."

"Nah, me neither. But he did it, all right, rest assured of that."

As I had come into the warehouse, I had been surprised by some guy I didn't know, stepping out in front of me. He was shorter than me, but broad, with a gray golf shirt stretched tight over muscle and a dead serious expression. His face looked like Yogi Berra sniffing bad egg salad.

He stood in my way there at the top of the center aisle and asked me could he help me. This of course meant that he didn't want to help me at all, that I wasn't getting any farther into the place unless we both agreed on my answer.

Instead of saying anything, I looked around the place for familiar faces. I didn't see even one; not a corner-boy in sight.

He asked me, "What'd you want?"

I said, "You mean right *now*, or in my life in general?"

"You wise?"

As an interviewer, this guy wasn't Bert Parks at Miss

America. I told him that I just wanted to speak to Albert, please, and he asked me to say my name. Then he asked if I had a business card. I grinned and looked around and shook my head at him. I said to this hatchet boy, "Look, just tell Albert that the guy who almost killed Buster Cook is out here waiting to see him. Please."

Muscles didn't say anything to that, just turned and went into the office, to come back out within thirty seconds, still looking serious. He brought his face up close to mine and he spoke very slowly, softly, evenly, but with meaning behind it. "Mr. Niklozak says *he's* the one almost killed Buster Cook."

He showed me something like a grin—but rotted teeth surrounded by pock-marked flesh diluted its warmth. I tried to smile back at him, and he led me into Albert's office.

Albert had about a hundred suits stacked in piles on the floor. He was down using a tiny pair of sewing shears to open each jacket and clip out the label, then do the same on the pants.

He looked away from the cloth just long enough to tell me, "Botany, they're all. I hate to do it, but it's become necessary. It breaks my heart."

I asked him, "Don't you have people to do this?"

"Oh, I got people." He gave me a disgusted glance, went back to his clipping. "I got people all right. Up the ass I got."

I asked him, "You want any help with that? I could help clip."

He said, "No. Get me a coffee."

I did, set it down on the floor by where he was working. I asked him, "Hey, Albert, what the hell was *that* all about?"

He didn't look up. "*What's* all about?"

I threw a thumb in the direction of the office door. The guy from outside had left. When Albert didn't answer, I said, "That big clipper, the guy who's screening your calls for you now, all of a sudden. He stopped me out there."

Albert stopped his snipping and looked up at me to say something. But before he started his answer, he said, "My

God, Tasti, you look awful. What's going on, you been sick?"

I just told him, "Just a lot of stuff. Too much. That's why I came in to see you. But who's the clipper?"

Albert let the tiny shears drop to his side. He leaned back against the paneled wall of the office. I got the idea that Albert wasn't doing much better than I was. He went back to work and said, "It's been nuts around here, Tasti, let me tell you. Sit down. Sit down. I been having more trouble this past month, more than ever, ever since I got the place."

I gave him a New York nod, to ask what was wrong.

"It's the business associates—past, maybe present, probably future, who God damn knows," he told me. "By the way, this—what I'm saying to you—it's all keep-your-mouth-shut stuff, right? I don't have to tell you that."

"No, right," I said. "It's the Yacovazzis bothering you?"

"Don't even say that. I'm a victim here, Tasti, of my own success. They want a big piece of everything, even my string."

"Your what?"

"My girls."

"Oh, yeah?

"Yeah. Since I started up this place, you know I been good about it. So now, now—this really hacks me off, I gotta tell you—just because I work hard, I build up a business, so I'm doing well, good, suddenly they want back in? The hand shake, the slap on the back, 'Good luck, Albert,' suddenly that don't mean shit? They want back in, not just the skim I been glad to give them since the beginning, but a hand in the operation too. *My* operation. So, suddenly I got some tough decisions to make. I got nine million things to be thinking about, to do around here—and I'm spending my time clipping labels—and I really gotta decide some stuff."

"That's why Bruno's outside screening your calls?"

"Mike. His name is. Yeah. As if *that's* gonna do any good. That's just cheesecloth in the wind, if they decide to come in. Why'm I even doing this for? Anyhow, anyhow, this is not a concern to you. Tasti, you look the worst I ever seen you. What's wrong? You been getting any sleep?"

"Yeah. No," I said, "I feel bad about telling you this now, though." I hadn't been thinking about Albert as a guy with troubles of his own.

"So tell me what. It's Annetta?"

"No, nah, that's fine. Kid's fine."

"Everybody's healthy again?"

"Yeah, that's all fine. Everything. What are your choices? With the business here?"

"Not too many." He didn't elaborate, so I didn't ask him to.

"Hey, but, Albert, people come in here once and you're not out front greeting them, like they're used to, they meet that big jerk instead, it's gonna cost you good will, isn't it?"

He said yeah, he knew. He told me that everything gets so damned complicated all the time. All he wanted to do was to deal his hot and cold goods and take care of his string of hot women, and no one would leave him alone to do that.

I told him how sorry I was to hear that. Told him he was looking good, I hadn't seen him in awhile. If greased-backed hair ever made a comeback, Albert would already be there, never having given up his Brylcreem or pocket comb.

He asked me if I needed another loan. He told me, "Whatever it is you need."

"Nah, I thank you. I gotta hold awhile on the pay-back, if you don't mind, but I don't need any more."

"Fine."

"Albert, look. I gotta talk to you about something bad. It seems like there's this girl."

He kept his glance on the material. He was picking out the tiny strands of thread using a gentle little move with his finger tips. "Yeah," he said, "it always seems like there's this girl, don't it."

"No, not like that. I'm good. It's that kid in my school, schoolgirl I told you about. She's crazy. She threatened to tell people that she and I, we had a thing, she even got knocked up by it. But none of this ever happened. I never touched her. She went crazy, that's all."

"What a minute," he said, "this is the one wanted you to plug her? In the bathroom? You told her no, thank God?"

"Yeah. Same one."

"I didn't tell you to get away from that? I didn't tell you all about Profumo and Christine Keeler, for Christ sake?"

"Yeah, you did. And I did. But she come up to me again. It was hard getting away."

"Oh, yeah, I'm sure."

"I didn't touch, Albert. I was good, you understand."

"Tasti, you never touched her?" Still working on the thread.

"Never."

Albert leaned away from his work and stretched his back, said "Aw, shit," like the muscles were hurting him. He stood up. He placed his hands onto the wooden-slatted chair behind his big wooden desktop. It was holding slipping stacks of inventory printouts, his coffee mug, a plastic hula dancer on a spring. "Not at anytime, you didn't? Just one time maybe? Tasti?"

"She took her bathing suit down in front of me. One time. I reached out my hand. I thought better of it right away. This I swear."

"She comes to school wearing a bathing suit? Things have changed that much since you and me had Sister Edelina in grammar school?"

"It was a class trip. Jones Beach. Completely legitimate."

"Hey, what'd'ya think Sister Edelina would look like in a bathing suit?"

"My God, Albert."

Albert looked down into his mug, went over, topped off the coffee from the giant aluminum maker on a card table in a corner of the office. He held up the coffee to me and asked, "You want a beer? I got an ice box out there." He used the mug to point through the office wall.

I shook my head. I was still trying to clear out Sister Edelina in a bathing suit.

Albert sat down behind his desk. He said, "Tasti, let me tell you something. I got fifteen girls to my name right now, all of them good girls now, some stay with me long time, some I have to rotate in and out. One thing. You don't have to tell me they are crazy. *I* know they're crazy. Girls like that, they all are. It's just a question of varying degrees, that's all. I can help you out, I'm sure. But I been real busy."

"Albert, you know me, I panic like crazy over shit like this."

"Yeah, you *look* crazy."

"I have to ask you, go over there, do what you must to get me out of this. I'm in trouble, and I got nobody else to ask. You see, it's gone too far. You know how to clean up messes like this, better'n I do. How to deal with it."

"Of course I do. I understand what you're saying. You just want your garbage picked up."

"Yeah, well, you know, just smooth things down for me, like you do. Please try."

"When'd you say you wanted me to do this?"

"Now. Right now. The sooner the better would be great."

In better times for us, there were no problems which couldn't be taken care of by two guys working together, by thinking about it for awhile, by laughing over it in the end.

"*Now*, you want?"

"Sure. That'd be great, Albert. Remember how the two of us together beat the Green Hornet?"

The Green Hornet was a pluperfect street kid whose real name was Benny "The Mutt" Kelleher. He was a few years older than us and he grew up in the Back Lots, out behind Duck Alley, in the shadows of Depressions and World Wars, loving every minute of it.

These days you can still find him sitting in the

Raspberry Lounge every afternoon on his way home from his job making boxes. Back in the fifties, he was a natural nemesis, a predator, but still, he was the one who had showed us how to peel off a beer label with the same hand you were using to hold the bottle.

He had been named The Green Hornet in honor of his pea green snap-brim cloth cap, his lime green jersey, dark green fatigue pants, and black sneakers. His wire-rimmed glasses had over the years branded permanent red lines across the ridge of his nose and along the sides of each of his white-walled temples. His upper arms could fit through napkin holders, the glasses had lenses that looked bullet-proof, but he could sure shoot the basketball. He had a razor perfect set shot—from out around three-point land, before there was such a place—and a deadly hook shot that he could shoot either lefty or righty, a shot which he could either bank in—after calling "Board!"—or sink straight—after calling "Swisher!"

Albert had foolishly once challenged him to a game of Horse; Albert and I formulated a brilliant strategy.

In the Armory, with a mob watching, Albert took the ball, dribbled twice, stepped back, drove, sank an awkward looking lay-up with the ball "tha-wanking" against the old wooden backboard as he yelled out, "Suckling!"

The Green Hornet took a step toward him. "What'd you call me?" He took back the ball.

"I didn't call you anything, jerk. That was my Restoration poets lay-up."

"What the hell you talking about?"

"You have to name a poet of the early seventeenth century as you sink the shot. Sir John *Suckling* was my choice." I'd been tutoring Albert.

Second shot, Albert sank a chippie and yelled, "Trinitroluene. That's my TNT shot, Mutt. The shooter's gotta give the chemical name of a powerful explosive as the ball is released." Albert always knew his explosives. "That's H-O, asshole."

The game went on like that until the final shot—Albert had named a substance that is secreted by the liver. "Glycogen."

The Hornet actually had a chance to win as he came up with an answer. "Wait a minute, wait a minute, wait just *one, fucking minute.* I fucking know that one! I fucking know that answer! We had that in school! The fucking liver secretes bile! Yeah, bile!"

But he missed the shot.

"You have to cut me a sprout here, Albert," I was saying to him in the warehouse office, where we were trying to be adults. "Remember we used to use that expression all the time? Albert, I'm asking you one more time—cut me a big sprout."

"Yeah, Tasti, I will. I'm real busy right now though."

"If it could be quick, done right away, it'd be great."

"Yeah, right as soon as I leave here then. I'll head over there. Do what it takes. You wanna come with me?"

"No. No, I can't, man."

"Don't worry about it. We both'll be okay with our troubles. We beat people by using our heads, don't we, Tasti? Instead of with our hands, right?"

I wasn't sure what he meant. I told him, "Sure we do. Like the Green Hornet, huh?"

"Like what?"

"Nothing." I moved toward the frosted glass of his office door.

Albert told me, "And so it will be, so it will be with this little girl of yours. So don't worry about it, fag-hole. Just get out of here. Don't worry about it. Your garbage, it'll get picked up."

May 20, 1961, in study hall:

"So she won't even go with you?"

"Nope, I guess not."

"She know you got nobody else?"

"I guess so. I'll get somebody else. I'm looking around."

"Yeah. How come she don't wanna go?"

"She wants to go, just not with me."

"Why not?"

"She just doesn't want to, that's all. I think maybe she's been fishing for somebody else to ask her. She got a dress. I don't know, maybe Carlie Gazoli or somebody. I saw her talking to him."

"Jeez, that's awful, that creep. Tasti, I gotta keep my mouth shut, because it's an area where I don't know."

"It's just something I have to work out for myself anyway. I'm surprised to hear you say that there's something you don't know anything about."

"Yeah, just with this one thing though."

"Girls. God."

"No, wait, not girls I don't know nothing about. I was just talking about this one particular instance. You and her, and her telling you no, she won't go. Girls in general, yes, I do know a little something about, there."

"Yeah."

"How about Maggie Doran? You want me to ask her for you?"

"Albert, I don't want any of your seconds. No, don't ask anybody for me. I'll never be THAT desperate, that I'll be taking your leftovers, for crying out loud."

"Then what are you telling me all this for? To help you out or no?"

"Nah, no, just to tell somebody. I don't know. I was just hoping for some—I don't know—insight. See? With me and her, things were okay, I kept waiting for it to get better. So instead it keeps getting worse. Now she leaves me out to dry like this."

"Okay, now listen—don't be offended—now let me ask you this one thing."

"No, I never made her."

"Oh, okay. Fine. I just ask, you know. My mind is often on the internal massage."

"Yeah, sure, that's okay. That's not it, though. Most of all it's just, I don't know, I just got feeling so damn sad about everything. Not complete somehow, I don't know. I feel bad for me, I feel almost as bad for HER, I don't even know why I should. It's like I'm not even complete and getting more like that, all the time."

"So what's gone wrong, you think, with you and her?"

"I don't know. It's sort of like, everybody's got to feel special once in awhile, you know, and we never did. I should try, I figured, but I don't even know how to do it. I tried sharing things with her, you know, telling her my feelings and stuff?"

"Don't do that. There's some things, a LOT of things actually, that just are not shared with the members of the opposite sex, not shared with NOBODY. SHOULD not be shared. Huh? Am I right? You know that. And what you have to convince yourself—so that you feel okay about it—it's this—that that's okay. That's good. Forget about it. Sharing ain't worth shit. Sharing is just crap, in most of the times. Feelings are okay, they're okay, but they were meant for just YOURSELF to feel them, not for anybody else. Let them get their own feelings. They can share THOSE if they want to."

"You think so?"

"Sometimes some chick'll say to me, 'Hey, I feel like we're gonna end up just living together, just sharing the rent. Nothing else.' So I tell her, 'Hey, that's fine. That's okay. Rent's meant to be shared.' It's one of those things.

But that's enough.   You wanted to share everything with everybody, you would've been, I don't know, you would've been born Siamese twins or something.   Am I right? Sometimes, Tasti, about some things, you just gotta stuff a rag and keep your damn mouth shut."

TEN

FRIDAYS, ESPECIALLY NICE Fridays in June, were notorious cut days at the high school. For seniors it was even worse. Arlynn Svenson's attendance had always been spotty anyway—fake-sick affected—so when I had found her name on the attendance list after school that Friday after I had gone to see Albert, I didn't give it much thought.

It had been a cold-for-June Thursday when I went to the warehouse to ask Albert to cut me a sprout. When he had assured me that my garbage would get picked up—that he'd get to it as soon as he left work—I knew his word was good. He was always a guy who liked to get to things quickly, so I figured by the next day, maybe he'd have things straightened out for me somehow, or at least he'd have a read on the situation.

How would he handle it? I didn't think about that too much. I could tell that he had been preoccupied with his Yacovazzi problems, but I figured he could still do me the fix. I was confident that he could.

I gave him Arlynn's name and address before I left the warehouse. He didn't want any directions.

I was anxious to see what sort of effect that his visit would have on Arlynn. I thought that I could check out her facial expression and body language without mentioning anything to her. I was disappointed and a bit relieved when she hadn't been in school.

I drove home and called Albert up at the warehouse, but they told me he had left. I phoned his house; there was no answer. I called twice more that night, still nothing.

That weekend I kept trying to work in a visit to Albert's, but Annetta kept us pretty busy. During our crowded weeks, we saved up a lot of things to do on the weekends. She had mapped out a picnic at Sunken Meadow for the three of us, and a visit to her family. She also had a list of jobs for me to do around the apartment. The landlord let us paint, as long as we supplied the materials and checked with him on color before we dipped the brush. The last tenants had worn sandals and beards and had painted the place black, just like in the Rolling Stones' song.

The next Monday I was anxious to get in to school—a concept that hasn't occurred to too many teachers in their career. That day I stood in the hallway outside my classroom door during each passing time, between every period, but again, I didn't see Arlynn at all. At three o'clock, her name was on the attendance list again.

I just wanted to go home and assume that my problem had been solved. My confidence had been going low-tide, high-tide for a couple days; now I had myself almost convinced that Albert had gotten things all fixed up for his old buddy.

Every man's son should believe that his father can fly, if only for a little while. I had started a campaign to convince James Albert that I had the power over gravity. I would hold my arms out and swoop down over the top of his crib and tell him, "Look, James, your daddy's flying. He's flying!"

I don't remember how this idea started, but it was all mixed up somehow with kids adoring super-heros and me adoring my son. I knew that, if successful, it would be an ego hoax of the first order, one that would come crashing down around me as the kid grew, but for awhile, I figured I'd be keeping company with Superman and Captain Marvel. Which was not bad company to be keeping.

I accepted the fact that as my son got bigger, the cracks in the stone wall of our relationship would also grow. I knew that there would soon come a time that he would think of me—as I had thought of my own father—as a guy who was lucky to just survive, a man barely holding onto his ability to clothe and clean and feed himself. A Buddha of the Back Porch.

But I figured for a little while at least, I should be able to stumble my way back home from my days filled with bad hops and wrong turns—to a person who though that his daddy could fly.

And I did fly once.

Remember. After I had been awakened from my sound hospital-corridor sleep to be told that I had a son living two floors above me, I took a walk and navigated the streets of Mineola, New York, with my boot-heels barely clicking on the pavement.

"Look, son, look, James Albert, daddy can fly. Whoa, Daddy's flying."

Flying can be dangerous though. I remember seeing a Jack Palance movie where he played a magician who had the populace of ancient Rome convinced that he could fly. Things were going along fine for Jack until he started believing his own scam and decided to take off from the top of some tower without his secret harness.

He didn't make it.

Two more phone calls to Albert's house that night—both unanswered.

Tuesday morning I looked into Arlynn's homeroom at 8:32 and I didn't see her.

Levittown was a manufactured town, nothing but a terrific idea one moment, then an actual place with 17,000 actual houses the next. It was thrown up in about a week and a half right after World War II, to give the boys coming back from the war houses to raise their families. Each place would cost them about five grand. People predicted that the town would be a slum within five years, but pride and faith in the future had made it into a pretty good place for kids to grow up.

Since all the house were cellar-less and built on old

potato fields, the rumor was that you could kick a hole in any of the sheet-rock walls and find potatoes still growing there in the dark.

I stopped by one of these houses on my way home after school on Tuesday. I had never met Arlynn's father before.

He held the screen door open, didn't ask me in, didn't react when I told him I was one of Arlynn's teachers. He was wearing a sleeveless undershirt, he had big ears and no chin, a couple days' worth of gray stubble on his sun-tanned face.

"Arlynn hasn't been in school," I told him. I was standing on his little cement front stoop.

"She never liked school," he said. He let it go at that.

"I was wondering if I could talk to her." A month ago, if someone had told me I'd be asking to talk to Arlynn, even my best sarcastic look wouldn't have covered it.

"The girl never liked school, never liked any of the kids there. Never liked anything."

"She, uh, yeah, she seemed unhappy a lot of the time. I noticed that."

"Probably didn't like you either, I'm guessing."

"Well, actually Arlynn and I managed to have a fairly positive relationship." Yeah, she took her bathing suit down for me. "I'd like to make sure she's going to graduate, that she has her sufficient credits and everything." I hated teachers talking like teachers.

"She told me she got all her credits."

"Well, Mr. Svenson, the year's not over yet. She still has finals to take."

"She always told me she was sticking around till she graduates, then she'd be off. Her mother's out in California. She's probably out there with her, where the movies are."

"Arlynn's no longer living at home then?"

"Not any more. I come home, she was gone, her clothes were gone. No notes. No good-byes. Good-bye."

"Mr. Svenson, when was this?"

"She did not like school, did not like Levittown. And she didn't like me. She told me that."

"Oh, no?"

"That's fine too. I'm glad she finished school, at least. That's important. She's gone then, her clothes're gone. She had some money from working. I wish her luck. No hard feelings."

"Her clothes were gone?"

He nodded.

"Mr. Svenson, do you have an address, where your wife, your ex-wife is? Or a phone number or something?"

"Nope. She'd always said she'd stick around to finish high school and then go. As far as I know, she's gone as far as she can go. Maybe out in California, she was always watching television and the movies. With her mother, maybe. Her clothes and a couple of suitcases left with her. She's glad to have them."

"I hope you hear something."

"But let me tell you this—Our Lord Jesus Christ knows where she is all right, doesn't He?"

"Sure."

The old guy's conversation got less cheery after that. He kept inching the screen door closed.

No notes, no messages? Nope.

No communication since, even with the former Mrs. Svenson? Nope.

Any regrets on the old man's part? None whatsoever.

As I turned to leave, he asked me to repeat my name. When I did, he told me, "I got something in here for you." He disappeared from the door. I stood on the stoop, looking at the mirror image house across the street and one down.

Arlynn's father came back and handed me a manilla envelope with a note scribbled across it. It said, "Mr. Tasti, Please think only good thoughts of me as you listen to this. Cooch."

The *i*'s of the note, of course, were dotted with hearts. Inside the envelope was a cassette tape. Its plastic case called it *Blaze*. By Herman's Hermits.

Arlynn wasn't there for any of her finals, which began later that week and went on until the next Monday.

My phone calls to Albert's warehouse were all answered by a secretary whom I didn't know, or by the goon Albert had hired to protect himself from the Yacovazzis. The secretary and the goon would never put Albert on the line for me.

Arlynn had needed only one course to graduate—American History—and she had enough credit in the class to pull a D-minus without taking the final. So her name was added to the list of graduates. She hadn't ordered a cap and gown, or any graduation announcements. She hadn't picked up her tickets to the graduation breakfast.

Arlynn Svenson graduated in absentia. Her name was read off across the speaker system of the gymnasium filled with risers and folding chairs and bleacher seats that were occupied by people looking uncomfortable but proud in their suits and Sunday dresses.

Bouquets of fresh flowers had been placed alongside the temporary stage and by the little table that held the diplomas. The place still smelled like a gym though.

The graduation address centered on friendship and its importance to each individual in the graduating class. "Allow yourself to be a friend to the world," the speaker said, "and let the world be *your* friend too."

A couple babies were crying as the speaker popped his words into the microphone. A little kid clomped across the gym floor, chased down by a father wearing cowboy boots.

Nobody seemed to miss Arlynn Svenson at all.

Sometimes teachers survive by counting down their days until the summer. They spend their school year often surrounded by unstable, frustrated, borderline-psychotic individuals—and that's just in the faculty room. But they remain convinced that next fall, after the respite, they will get to shrug off all the failures of their past and they will get another chance to start all over again, from scratch. Each new year they can walk into classrooms with clean desktops and with colorful, new bulletin boards and they can tell themselves, "Maybe I'll get it right this time."

Preparing myself for that attitude, my summer plans were to paint two houses, take a course at Hofstra, and to get some Ozzie and Harriet time in with Annetta and James Albert.

My state of mind fluctuated from near ecstasy to night-sweating terror. I still hadn't spoken to Albert.

I called him at home two nights in a row and let the phone ring ten times. Finally he answered. I said, "Albert," and he hung up on me. I was going to call him right back, but I couldn't get myself to re-dial the number. Instead I just went to bed.

As a little kid, trying to make the switch from crib to grown-up bed, I had fallen onto the floor a hundred and eighty-seven straight nights. Then, after one successful stay-in-bed night, I had, like Joe DiMaggio and his hitting streak, started a new streak of twenty-seven nights crashing asleep onto the floor.

One morning at the end of June I drank a pot of coffee and went out to make a call from a booth. Albert's stooge answered. I didn't give him any lines about killing Buster Cook this time; I just told him that I absolutely had to talk to the boss.

He put down the phone for awhile, then came back on and told me that Mr. Niklozak was unavailable. I hung up the phone and drove over there.

That night I lay in bed with my upper arm blackened and aching. Annetta wanted me to go to the emergency room, or at least to a doctor in the morning. She told me that it could be dislocated. I said no, it was just a bruise. I wouldn't tell her what had happened, didn't even make up a cover story.

At least it was my left arm, so the next day, I could go out to the garage and fire the Pennsy Pinkie into the boards. I did that twice, for at least a couple hours each time. The second time, I didn't quit throwing the ball until it got too dark.

July 9, 1954, up in a tree:

"C'mon, Albert-Albert-Albert, tell."
"No, no, uh-uh, it's a secret."
"C'mon, you can tell me."
"Go ask somebody else."
"You the only one who knows. So, c'mon, tell me, please."
"Uh-uh."
"Why not?"
"Cause if I tell you, then I told somebody."

ELEVEN

DURING THE VIETNAM era, I served alongside a tough, shy American Indian named Quintana. He was short and stocky and had been in the ring. He used to grind his teeth when he slept, loud enough to be heard throughout the barracks. None of us speculated about what that meant, other than there must have been within him something that went beyond our shared general frustration and discomfort for the military life.

His hair was Indian straight and Indian black, combed back hard from the forehead. The hair was short by the standards of the time, but long by the standards of USAF Regulation 35-10. At guard-mount one evening before a swing shift, our NCOIC stopped his inspection walk in front of Quintana, looked him left and right, stepped back, and told him to get a haircut.

Even though I was spending most of my duty-days up in Pass and ID, typing up cards, we were all officially Security Policemen and therefore safekeepers of the last bastion of spit'n'polish gung-ho-ery in the Force. The guys in Field Maintenance and Food Service and Supply might be getting away with wearing ratty fatigues and love beads, but not us, not the SP's.

First-Sergeant Maley—his hair follicles singed with a blow torch for that close-cropped look—had told us as we processed in, "I don't give a damn if you're AWOL, if you deserted, or if you're found lying dead on the flight line, your boots *will* be highly polished and your fatigues *will* be highly pressed and starched."

When Quintana was ordered to get a haircut, he didn't say anything. But neither did he get the haircut.

The next evening, the NCO repeated the order. This was during the time when hair length was all tied up with things like politics and pride and heritage. So Quintana just stared straight ahead.

The NCO—I can't remember his name—was an honest and hard-working tech sergeant whom we liked. He was neither a boot-licker nor a back-stabber, and we considered him a "lifer," which was a classification just below "career man" and above "maggot," the lowest form of military lowlife. Only George Washington and maybe Eisenhower had been "career men."

When this NCO mentioned the haircut to Quintana for the third straight guard-mount, he also mentioned something about an Article 15 and a court-martial, and we all believed him. Quintana just stood there at attention, thinking his thoughts into a corner somewhere.

That night I tried to talk to Quintana about it. He called the NCO an "Indian inspector," and he said, "I been to their schools, memorized their rules."

All of us waited anxiously for Quintana to show up for guard-mount the next evening and when he did, we let out a communal curse-word of shock. His temples were whitewashed, buzzed even closer than Sgt. Maley's.

Later, I got Quintana alone and I asked him—by holding my palms up and pulling down the corner of my mouth—"So what'd you do?"

He looked at me awhile, smiled, took a look around, and then flipped off his fatigue cap. Out poured a cascade of hair, falling beyond his ears on the sides, over his collar in the back.

He told me, "They can do what they want to the sides, my friend, the top belongs to me."

I've always liked that line. It speaks to me of balancing dignity, discipline, and personal freedom. Stories I've heard of the Brown Shoe War center on the American fighting man's advantage over his German or Japanese counterpart because of his ability to think for himself and to improvise, to keep a portion of himself as his alone.

America is a country stocked by people like Quintana and Albert Niklozak, a country stuffed full of Indians and prisoners, immigrants and policemen and vagrants, high school students and middle-level managers who can all say, "They can do what they want to the sides, my friend, the top belongs to me."

"Tasti, let me ask you something. Have you ever known me to ever be affiliated with the Avon?"

"With what? No."

"Have I ever, as far as you know, been known to manufacture, represent, or repair these products? Avon Corporation products? Skin care? Eye line? Anything at all like that?"

"No. What are you talking about?"

"So why the fuck are you busting into my house middle of the night, you're waking me up, acting like we're the Avon girls, huh? I'm talking about, you came to me, you ask me to do you a favor, take care of something for you, fix it up, which I did. *Which I did.* But now you want it both ways, it sounds to me like. You fucking knew at the time I wasn't no Avon lady, but you were, am I right?"

"Albert."

"No. You knew. You knew who it was you was asking. And what you were asking for. This is no fucking Lollipop Farm, Kiddy City, buddy. You know about me, what I do. I fence. I pimp for fun. I *talk* muscle some times so I don't have to *use* muscle. Sometimes, though, I have to use it too. What are you here for, asking me? Just shut up and stay the hell away from me. I don't like how you operate."

"I'm here, Albert, I'm just asking."

"What'd you expect? What'd you expect me to do?"

"I don't know."

"You. You're a guy, you go all to shit and crazy when he's faced with something he don't like, he can't handle. Then, after it's all over and done with, taken care of, now he's pretending again he's Mickey Rooney or somebody. You ain't no Avon Lady, pal, so forget about it. You're bloody all over, just like the rest of us. Pretending you ain't don't make it so."

"I'm just asking you—I'm not accusing anybody—I'm not making any claims. All I know, Albert, I'm asking you if anything happened that I should know about when you went over to Arlynn's. Albert. I don't want you to talk about anything you don't want to talk about. I *know* it was me asked you for the favor. I appreciate it. I know it was *me* came through the doors of your place of business, and you obliged. Like an old friend would. This I appreciate. You cut me a sprout. I remember coming in through those doors there with that specific phrase in mind. Now all of a sudden you're talking about muscle, how you use it and things. *You* brought that up. Not me. If you don't want to talk about that, okay then, that's fine too."

"Oh. Oh, so I see. You know who it is you sound like now? You know who you sound like? Fucking Pontius Pilot. Fucking Pontius Pilot washing his hands of the whole matter. 'Hey, it ain't me, babe, it ain't me, Jews. I am not involved.' Jesus Christ, that's what I mean all the time about things getting so confusing. How can you be such an asshole and still manage to live with yourself every day?"

"Albert, let me ask you, so how come you didn't let me talk to you, at the warehouse, or on the telephone calls? You don't wanna talk to your old friend anymore, huh? I had to sneak in here, middle of the night, to see you. Why's that, Albert? Why?"

"I didn't wanna talk to you."

"I wind up getting my arm half twisted off."

"That's too bad about that, that was a misunderstanding. I already talked to Mike about that."

"Oh, thanks, so now he won't twist off my other arm."

"That was *your* decision, jerk. Tasti, listen, you never *once* came in there, just left a message for me, 'Thank you, Albert, I appreciate what you did for me.' That would have been less confusing. Than this."

"What do you mean? I called you up. I called you up all the time. Here and at the warehouse. I couldn't get through."

"So you decided to come down here now to make sure there's no blood been splattered on your pretty, white, chalk-dust white, fucking schoolteacher hands, right? You can touch her tits, but you can't touch her blood, is that right?"

"I never touched anything. Albert, all I'm asking you is, what happened? What happened when you went over there?"

"I went over there. That's all you have to know, pal. You asked me to go over, so I went over there."

"No, Albert, that's not all I have to know. I have to know what happened. I have to know what got done over there."

"You cocksucker, listen to me. I get so tired of putting up with you. I did what you told me to do. Why you so concerned now? After the fact."

"Albert, where'd she end up? What the hell is the story?"

"She's still giving you trouble? Is she still threatening to sound off about you getting in her bathing suit there on the beach?"

"No, she's not."

"Of course not. So, you see, you're all set. Why don't you just get out of here? Don't ask me no more favors. Go on, go, get out of here."

"You gonna call up your goon to come over here, to throw me out? C'mon. C'mon, Albert, can't we just talk about it, without getting ourselves all upset?"

"No. Look, Tasti, you asshole you, I don't need Mike or anyone else if I want you gone out of here. If I want, I myself can twist your fucking arm right the hell off your body and hand it to you. I think *that* point we established, years ago from now."

"Albert, what'd you do over there?"

"Why you keep asking?"

"I'm concerned."

"She's not around."

"Where'd she end up?"

"Oh, yeah, I forgot, I'm her fucking truant officer too, I forgot that. Tasti, I'm getting sick of this."

"Well, so am I, Albert."

"Tasti, just what'd you expect from me? Huh? Why ain't you happy? Why ain't you ever just happy?"

I didn't have any answer to that.

As I was leaving his place, Albert said to me, "Tasti. Don't come around here no more. I don't wanna see you."

I nodded an okay to him.

"I mean here or at the warehouse too."

I nodded again. He had asked me, "Why ain't you ever just happy?"

There were so many things I did not want Albert to tell me, so much I had to force myself to ask. There was so much I didn't want to hear. There was so much he didn't want to tell me. The top belonged to him.

I was out in the alley, spending hours throwing a stupid pink rubber ball against the garage wall, trying for answers. Or else lying cold-sweat awake next to my wife, hours at a time, middle of the night, our son curled asleep in his crib in the next room, me just lying there sweating up the sheets. Trying to think, Albert, just to think. Checking the numbers on the clock by the bed, every couple minutes. Listening to my wife breathing. Trying to figure out what must have happened.

Let me see, this: Arlynn's home from school. She's alone, watching her soap operas, she goes to answer the bell. It's Albert standing there.

He's into his Big Daddy Pimp role, playing it right up. Right away Arlynn's scared of him, but she lets him come into the house anyway. He's a man, looking strange, acting different, a plot device for her, coming right in off the street. And she's a girl craving adventure, any adventure. He'll do. She can't figure out why he's here. She doesn't ask; doesn't care. Something tells her she's into something good.

He talks to her, quiet, gets to know who she is, what she wants out of things, what she likes, what kind of plans she's made for her life. My name doesn't come up.

Nobody's ever asked her to talk about herself before. She's amazed about how great her day is turning out. Albert's the whoremonger, she's impressed. Albert's the Enforcer, she's Lolita. Right here in her own living room. Her father's gone to work.

She gets them a couple drinks from the old man's liquor cabinet, mixing them, pretending she knows what she's doing.

She comes on to this guy, yeah, she'd do that. Nothing too strong, maybe a hiked up leg, or looking at him while she's lighting up a cigarette, trying to say sexy lines she remembered from some movie she saw. Pretending to stretch, trying to get her tits to stick out underneath what-ever it is he's caught her wearing that day.

She's letting the guy know how much she wants it. But Albert, he's got no time for that. He's got a whole string of girls working for him, has access anytime he wants. They're better than this and almost as young. He's more concerned with getting back to the warehouse and fighting off the Yacovazzis, keeping his share of the business. He's just here doing a quick favor for a friend.

Plus, this girl's bait, so he lays off. Please tell me you lay off, Albert.

So he starts sliding into his strong-arm talk, he's letting her know that she's really getting some people mad at her, and scared too. And when people get mad, and scared, they react poorly. It could be dangerous.

Arlynn's still miffed that he didn't pick up on her invitation to screw. Plus, she doesn't like to be threatened.

She goes into one of her fits, like in the principal's office when he was trying to get her to go home. Now, for Albert, she's screaming, crying, kicking furniture, maybe even taking a swipe at him.

But here's the thing. This doesn't impress Albert at all.

He's seen it a thousand times, with his girls. Doesn't mean anything. Doesn't get him upset. It certainly doesn't cause him to lose his temper and go after her. At the very worst, *at the very worst*, he grabs an arm, maybe twists the skin, maybe a quick open-handed slap. Just to get her attention. Just to get her calmed down.

Arlynn sees how calm and in control this guy is. The thought hits her—this is not a guy to hack around with. He's no pansy-assed high school administrator, can't impress *this* guy. Yeah, she's figuring, this is no game. I could get my face messed up here, my beautiful face, by making people like this mad at me. What did I do to deserve this?

Albert probably didn't even have to touch her. Didn't even have to grab her arm, or take her face in his hand, between his thumb and strong fingers. Albert. Just the words, just the threats.

Then he puts some money on the table. How much? How much would Albert give her? Five-hundred? A thousand? He tells her he's heard that the Southwest is blossoming, everything's happening down there, since air-conditioning. Long Island swelters and it sucks.

She decides, a quick decision—Hey, I'm done with high school. I hate it here. Hate it all, everything within a hundred-mile radius. Why not just go? She looks into his face there. He's watching her think—she can't decide if it's menacing or kindly. It's both, she figures, it's both at the same time.

She thinks—Why not just go? For a couple months, a couple years, for good. The school year's almost over, she hates it anyway, she knows she can graduate no matter what.

He walks toward her from across the room, gives her a kiss that lasts a full minute, full of tongue and touching. He tells her Europe's nice too.

She says, "Oh, Europe, wow. I love Herman's Hermits. The group, you know? Everybody else's gone on, thinks they're gone by, but I still love them. I loved them since before junior high school. And they're English, that's Europe."

Albert tells her, "Yeah, they'd be over there. You could go see them. Cost you a little more, the plane and everything." He throws another thousand on the table.

After Albert's gone, she looks into the mirror in her bedroom, she says to herself, "Arlynn, darling, why not just leave all of this?"

She was scared of Albert, whoever the hell he was—but now she's not thinking about him at all, maybe not even putting much reality into it, she's lied so much about so many things. Maybe he wasn't even real. Just another one of her lies. But the money is still truly there, right tight in her hand.

She's anxious to get started with her new life. "No, not my *new* life, because I never really had an old one until now. I'm starting my *life*."

She packs up her clothes in her father's old suitcases, handles the stash of bills that Albert gave her, adds a couple bucks of her own from her job at the diner, and she's gone for good. She's gone west, gone to Hollywood, gone out to her mother, gone to South America, Europe, the newly air-conditioned Southwest, gone who knows where. Just gone. For good, that's all. For everybody's good.

She goes and she leaves us—me—she leaves me alone forever. She's out of it. We're out of it. It's over. It's over. And Albert did it by using his head, not muscle, right? Just like how he beat the Green Hornet at Horse, right? Peaceable and lawful.

"Is that it, Albert? Is that what happened to Arlynn? What, Albert? What?"

" . . . Yeah, that's what happened . . . if that's what you want."

Three o'clock in the morning, I was out in the alley, throwing the ball against the garage until a gasoline truck-

driver who lived one house over—he had to get up early—
leaned his head out the window to tell me to shut up.

Albert had asked me, "Why aren't you ever just
happy?"

Then he had said to me, "Don't come around here no
more. I don't wanna see you."

July 6, 1957, on the bulkhead:

"Hey, Tasti."
"What?"
"Let's do something. The both of us."
"Yeah, okay. There's nothing to do."
"C'mon, let's do it anyway. C'mon."
"What?"
"Huh?"
"Do what?"
"We hook down Cookie's house, c'mon."
"You mean like you said, with the chain? You mean it?"
"Yeah. Let's. We'll get everybody, try it."
"You're nuts."
"Yeah. No. C'mon, let's."
"You're nuts."
"Yeah."
"Yeah, but, Albert, suppose they catch us?"
"They won't catch us."
"Suppose they do?"
"If they do, we just deny it."
"What, all we do is just tell them it wasn't us? C'mon "
"Yeah, that's all. Deny it."
"They'll get us for it."

"How can they get us? Just remember—deny it, deny it, your friends deny it too. No one lets on. It's like the chain. If there's no weak parts to the chain, it doesn't break."

"You're nuts. You mean, just no one lets on and they have to let us go for it?"

"That's right. That's right. Hey, Tasti, haven't I ever taught you something? You gotta remember, you get caught at something, just stuff a rag. At all costs, just stuff a rag.

And keep your mouth shut. Don't say anything, don't say nothing, no matter where you are, what's happening. Just shut up. Make like you're better than them."

"Oh, yeah, Albert, when I'm caught."

"Yeah, Tasti, that's right. That's all you gotta remember. It's easy to do. You see Purple Heart *on* Million Dollar Movie? *Almost as good as* A Walk in the Sun, *and a lot more instructional. Even if the Japs wake you up in the middle of the night, a hundred times in a row, you just don't know nothing, and you're fine. All your friends are fine too."*

"Yeah, sure. This ain't the movies."

"Deny, deny, be a stand-up guy."

"Oh, jeez, now you're very poetic, darling."

"Yes. Yes, I am. I'm like that word we had on the vocabulary list. I'm very . . . I forget what it starts with. It's a word."

"You're poetic."

"No."

"Ignorant."

"No. Not that. It was on the list. About number, around number a hundred, around there. 'Area-dite.' I am very, very area-dite."

"Erudite."

"Yup. It means I always got the right word."

"Like erudite."

"Like deny."

"Deny, deny, be a stand-up guy?"

"Now you got it, fag-hole. I'm finally teaching you something."

"Yeah."

"Yup. But do you understand? Let me ask you, you understand?"

TWELVE

ABOUT FIFTY MILES north of Duck Alley, upstate in Newburgh, New York, right off the Thruway, sit two huge pre-fab industrial buildings. Each has a full, wall-high, white sunburst on the front, and an equal size white sign that says "Sunburst of Mountainville." Each of the buildings houses a factory.

A third building, smaller and using more glass, carries an identical logo but with no writing on its side. This building holds the offices of the Sunburst of Mountainville Corporation. The buildings seem out of sync with their rural surroundings. If one of the Sunburst workers, on break, would sit at a window and gaze out, like my dad had done from our back porch, this worker would look out at farmers' fields gone to scrub brush. Three or four clusters of giant weeping willows are sprinkled around the south end of each building. A stream cuts across the front property, equidistant from the Thruway and the building face.

Each building is busy but quiet. Fifty yards behind them, and down a steep cut in the landscape, a person could stand and be completely unaware of the little industrial park. Two young men, drunk, carrying shovels and a dog wrapped in a blanket, could bury that dog with no one to see them do it.

Standing there, they could hear the sound of the traffic heading north to Albany and south to the city and to Jersey. But that sound would be the only hint that it was the twentieth century.

The upstate springtime had been the wettest in at least twenty years, with not even one day's break between the big-flaked sugar-snow of late winter and the cold drizzle of April. The landscape had been washed out into a different look by the wet.

140

The roots of some medium-sized trees—willows and maple—had been unable to hold their grasp in the mud on the inclined earth, and they became uprooted and had fallen over. Their roots were now twisted up into the air. Burrow holes were punched into the earth by some small animal, through the dead, wet leaves and the soggy black dirt. Parts of the tree trunks had turned white, other parts to dark and rotted punk. The bark had been curled back or peeled off.

Mud had washed across the top of the scrub grass and stopped it from turning springtime green. Thin branches, twisting damply up toward the gray sky, jiggled a bit whenever the wind came.

Rocks and metals that had been buried for centuries had now been uncovered by the moving waters. Moss and lichen had yet to take their places on the granite faces. Grays and reds saw the sky for the first time since their inception.

Curling across the decaying leaves were a few strands of barbed wire, left over from some forgotten farm back when this was grazing land.

A thing still recognized as a human hand reached up out of the mud as if trying to grab the air.

Later, I made myself look at the black and white scenes. I leaned forward to them on the desk and, looking hard through the beginning of tears, I could see coming up out of the mud—the hand.

The next school year after Arlynn Svenson graduated was a quiet one for me. The gods of the guidance department had smiled on me and I had been blessed with small- to average-sized classes and only a few students who could reach up and try to kill at any minute.

Actually, in all my classroom years I had only one knife pulled on me, and that was by a parent at Back to School Night, intending to clean his nails during my presentation.

At home, Annetta and I were enjoying being witness to

141

the growth of our son. On the first nice weekend in April of that school year, we took him to a petting zoo behind Adventurer's Inn. There we joined a circle of maybe twenty other parents and kids surrounding a zoo-lady who had stacked up three fairly small, dark cages.

James Albert sat cross-legged in my lap, leaning back into my chest, and Annetta sat on the dirt to my right. The zoo lady told us that we would start by all petting a baby chick. She reached into the first cage and took out the chick, passed it to a little curly-headed girl who passed it on. James Albert and I both smiled as I took the little puff of poultry. I held it out for James Albert to touch. He moved one small finger across its head and I passed the bird on to Annetta.

The zoo-lady told us that next would be a bunny. We repeated the process and James Albert's smile and his eyes both widened. He stroked the bunny's ears.

My talk with Albert at his apartment the June before seemed a long way off. As far as I could tell, no one had heard from Arlynn in that year; and Albert and I had not spoken. I had only seen him once during that time—at a high school basketball game. He had looked at me, looked away, didn't say anything.

For a moment that snub reminded me of how I missed the way that we used to treat each other—with comfort and humor, mixed with respect. But my reverie was quickly replaced by a flash of anger at how he had reacted to everything.

I remembered standing over him in his apartment, almost yelling down at him as I begged him to tell me that everything was all right. I remembered that he had told me that things always got complicated.

The zoo-lady had finished her talk about chicks and bunnies. She reached into a third box and—I swear to God—here's what she pulled out: a twelve-foot boa constrictor.

She smiled at the circle of parents and kids as the snake

curled itself around her arm. Then she started passing it directly toward me. As this gruesome green-and-black killer got within three little kids of me and my son, I checked out faces in the circle. Adult and kid alike sat with expectant smiles. There was none of the mass panic that I figured had to be coming. If the panic did indeed come, I was ready to be its leader. But even my eighteen-month old son sat still and confident in my lap. I knew that for his sake I had to gut it out. I looked at Annetta, who smiled back at me. I looked at the snake. The snake looked right at me.

Now the zoo-ey was telling the crowd that we should learn to treat reptiles gently, hold them securely, and they would never hurt us. I had seen enough Tarzan movies back at the Nazbeth Theater to know what these things did to their prey. They would wrap their bodies—which were just one giant long muscle—around their victim's neck and squeeze until the top of your head exploded into a gray and red mist.

The boys and girls in the petting circle were told that they were passing the snake along too quickly. If it caught up with the bunny or the chick, each of them would be no more.

I had always believed that snakes belonged under rocks and in bad dreams. The zoo-lady was saying that they were not slimy feeling, as people always expected them to be, but instead that they felt exactly like a rubber garden hose.

I took the snake and quickly passed it onto Annetta, who was enjoying my discomfort.

"See?" she whispered to me, "It *does* feel like a rubber garden hose. Now that you've held it once you'll never be afraid to touch snakes again."

"Yeah," I told her back, "but I'm never going to pick up another rubber garden hose as long as I live."

We both looked up into the sky as a few droplets of rain speckled our shoulders.

Upstate it was raining harder—much harder.

Later, I made myself look at the black and white pictures. I leaned forward over them on the desk and, looking hard through the beginning of tears, I could see coming up out of the mud—the hand and its wrist.

The rain washed the dirt off many things that spring, but as always, most things stayed buried.

Naj Bimbaghulya's husband, Uncle Frank, stayed buried in his final resting place. Albert's severely goitered, crazy aunt had joined her husband; and their daughter, Archanjela, had solved the puzzle of their treasure hunt once and for all. She visited both graves each Mother's Day, Father's Day, and around Christmas. She always wound up laughing and crying at the same time.

The Indian who had been disinterred from Nassau Knolls so that he could join his wife in Florida stayed buried down there, as far as I know. His suit and his bones rested peacefully a few miles to the east of Disney World, where you could stand and listen to the moving water.

The Shadow, the nearly blind and deaf dog that Albert had shot as I had held and petted it—with Albert and me drunk and crying— stayed buried near the upstate camp where we had stood and then sat down and drank and talked, and then finally made up our minds. The dog was buried a few hundred yards behind Sunburst of Mountainville. We had taken turns digging, working the tip of the shovel to dig out the boulders that got in our way. We wanted the Shadow's grave to be deep enough to stay down and undisturbed forever.

Someone digging alone, to bury a body, might get impatient and stop the digging as soon as he hit the first ledge of granite.

The half-emptied bottle of Beefeaters gin that Albert and I had buried by the end of the boardwalk at Jones Beach stayed two feet down in the sand. The shoreline caught most of the storms coming up the Atlantic coast that spring, but the sand seemed to find a way of shirking off the ravages of hard-pounding water that clay and mud couldn't bring themselves to do.

So most things stayed buried that spring.

But some things did not.

Later, I made myself study the black and white photographs. I leaned forward over them on the green metal desktop and, looking hard through the beginning of tears, I could see coming up out of the mud— the hand and its wrist. And maybe part of a face.

Albert's uncle's property—where we had built the camp—butted up against the property owned by the Sunburst of Mountainville Corporation. We would take Exit 17 onto Route 52 toward Fishkill and then hook back into the woods and hills to get there.

We had walked under the branches of pine trees and then skidded down the side of a gully and buried the Shadow in the cut of land behind the two factories and the one-floor office building.

Albert also had business dealings with Sunburst. They made fireworks, which were Albert's favorite product line, and he would go upstate just to buy some surplus from them at a cut rate. Each November, when he went north to hunt, he would stop by the Sunburst offices, sometimes just to keep his face in front of them, in case a good deal ever came up during the year.

The Sunburst of Mountainville Corporation was Albert's corporate supplier, and its property acted as Albert's burial ground.

I met Bobby Gallaga one night in a bar in Roslyn. Over the jukebox and the crowd noise, I asked him if he had gone upstate to hunt with Albert that past fall. He told me no, that he hadn't been up to that camp of Albert's ever. He said, "Albert still goes up to Newburgh a couple times a year though. Sometimes when it's not even hunting season."

I said, "Oh, yeah?"

He asked me, "You and Albert don't see much of each other any more, huh?"

I shook my head.

He said, "You don't even come by the warehouse any more."

I told him I had a lot of new stuff going on in my life, I didn't have time for crap like that.

Gallaga said to me, "Oh, big shot, huh?"

Even as a kid, Gallaga had been the type to enjoy telling someone, "Ou, that fingernail looks bad, you're gonna lose it."

Later, I made myself keep looking at the black and white pictures. I leaned forward over them on the desk and, looking hard through the beginning of tears, I could see coming up out of the mud— the hand and its wrist. And the partially decomposed face of Arlynn Svenson.

❖

February 17, 1972, in a place in Queens:

"They got Bobby Gallaga's father on a Lew and Lavvie again. I heard it was Bobby dimed him this time. I'm not saying that was right, but they should ass-can the old maggot, certainly. Cut off his balls, stuff 'em in his mouth, right?"

"So that's how they execute people now? Balls in the mouth? I didn't realize. Albert, a lawyer, he might go for 'cruel and unusual' on that."

"It wouldn't be unusual if they did it all the time, to all these creeps. So hey, pardon me, so I'm being Pollyanna here. World'd be better off without some of these fucking freaks around. Charlie Starkweather, guys like that? You kidding me? Burn 'em all."

"Well, I don't know."

"I'm weeding the garden, Dad, just weeding the garden. Excuse me for being concerned."

"Well, maybe. But you know what's wrong with Gallaga's father, and those kinda guys?"

"Yeah, I do."

"They are of the age of Muhammad Ali, instead of Joe DiMaggio."

"Tasti, what the hell you talking about now? Sports?"

"Yeah, I'm talking about responsibility to the society, to the team, to the world, to the concept, instead of just to the individual, to the ego. The whole history of this country's century of society is brought out by these two guys. First part of this century, we all wanted to be like Joltin' Joe. Now every poor kid and everybody wants to be like Ali."

"You drunk?"

"No, you?"

"No. I don't want to be like Ali, that's what he's calling himself, once used to be Cassius Clay."

"You're not a kid, that's why you don't wanna be him. Back with DiMaggio, it was grace and style back then, it was down-play yourself."

"So you say, down-play yourself, so a man's first debt is to his fellow man, before to himself?"

"Yes, it is. A debt he owes to the world for being allowed to live in it."

"No, it's not. It's to his OWN morality, at least it is if'n he's got one. A debt to his own well-being and peace of mind only."

"YOU drunk?"

"No, you?"

"So personal morality holds the highest position? Over society?"

"Absolutely. Sure it does."

"Whatever it happens to be? If Hitler's personal morality told him—kill all the Jews—then he was supposed to do that?"

"Yes. But it was the job of the rest of the world of society to stop him."

"Because their personal morality was different than his."

"Certainly. But also because the man was an asshole."

"Assholes are to be treated differently?"

"Absolutely. Yes. They should be treated like assholes. All the time."

"So in my theory, you'd say Ali is right. If it was between Ali and Joe."

"Yeah. Man looking to better himself is the geese of our wheels."

"What? 'Grease,' you moron, not 'geese.' And you're not drunk?"

"Nope. I'm not."

"See, Albert, as you know, I always liked Sonny Liston, so mostly I don't like Ali because of that."

"I understand."

"You can't like 'em both. It's like Dean Martin and Jerry Lewis. They split up, you gotta choose one, go with that one."

"Yeah, that thing, you even told me once, it even goes on to the second generation."

"Yup, it does. I chose to back Dino initially, not Jerry, so when their kids got rock bands, I had to go with Dino, Desi, and Billy, instead of Gary Lewis and the Playboys."

"Tasti, you ARE loyal, that's one thing I gotta hand you."

"Yes, I am."

"Fair enough."

"But what you said about a man's personal morality taking the top of the heap? Over all else?"

"Yeah?"

"Sounds promising. I'll take that under advisement."

"That's all I ask."

"Yeah, I will. But nothing's ever simple, right? You always tell me that. If it's just you and the rest of the world, if you do everything for yourself, you're a psychotic. You do everything for everybody else, you're a saint, which is just as bad. Saint or psychotic."

"No, because you do things all the time for yourself that won't come back to get you in the long run. You don't kill someone who pisses you off because then they'll get you for it in the end. Just like they got Hitler. Maybe. MAYBE they got him, we're not a hundred percent sure. They never did find him in the bunker."

"And that's the only reason you don't kill somebody? Cause society'll get you for it in the end?"

"Yeah. Just about."

"You're either drunk or psychotic."

"Admittedly, it gets all a bit confusing at this point."

"It's crazy."

"It's nuts."

"But, personal morality, huh? I'll take it under advisement. Albert, friend, I'll definitely take it under advisement."

"Friend, that's all I'm asking."

THIRTEEN

BOBBY GALLAGA HAD dimed his own father and I had to decide if I would dime my best friend. Personal morality, the good of society. Dean or Jerry, DiMaggio or Cassius Clay. Second generation loyalty. Psychotic or saint. To forget the whole thing or to betray Albert, I had to decide.

Let me tell you about Bob and Ray, how funny they were.

After teaching school each day I faced a forty-five minute drive home on the Wantagh and Northern State Parkways. Bob and Ray were doing their afternoon radio show, on WNEW I think it was. I couldn't always listen to it; I'd have to turn it off sometimes.

My eyes would begin to tear up and my shoulders would shake and my right-side tires would start catching the outside crack in the pavement. Bob and Ray were *that* funny, almost *too* funny; they were almost dangerous.

It was on a news break from their show that a voice that sounded like Wally Ballou's told me that a partially decomposed body had been found buried upstate and had been identified as a Long Island teenager who had been estranged from her family for almost a year but had never been reported missing.

I kept my eyes on the road. I did not turn off the radio, and the announcer sent it back to Bob and Ray. I listened to them for the rest of the ride home.

The next day, burning up a fake sick day, I drove up the Thruway and across Route 52, and then I walked across a cut field to the muddy patch of gully where the body had been found. I had stopped at a diner for directions, but I could have found that place by myself.

Only one cop was there, in uniform; he was smoking a pipe. Yards of yellow tape hung from the trees and the bushes, like a May Pole celebration. I was surprised to see people; maybe six or seven curious locals stood in groups and talked quietly. Two teenagers laughed with each other, then looked around, got quiet again. I talked to a man and his wife who told me they had driven over from Rhinebeck. I let them keep their impression that I was a reporter. Some other visitors probably thought that I was a gore freak; most just didn't notice me. There were more riveting sights than me to be viewed and spoken about in quiet tones by these lumber-jacketed neighbors.

Death didn't come like this very often up here. When it did, it made the papers for a week, and more; it got spoken about at supper. The death place got its share of visitors.

I avoided the cop, who seemed bored and cold and unwilling to talk to anyone. My shoes slid across the mud on the uneven, puddled ground. I got as close as I could. I kept twisting in circles and looking at the trees and rocks and up at the sky.

Just a hole in the ground. I wondered how much of her had been left, after all this time. How long does it take before a body is just bones and clothes, like the old Indian that I watched them disinter from his grave at Nassau Knolls. Burned by the acids of the earth.

Later, giggling and teary-eyed, I drove back down to the Island listening to Bob and Ray as soon as I could pick up their station. They were selling advertising space on the metallic side of the Bob and Ray satellite, which was designed to orbit only twenty-eight feet above the earth.

That evening, after pounding the rubber ball harder than I ever had before into the clattering side of the garage—for two numbing hours—I finally stopped when I knew that it wasn't doing me any good. I caught the last bounce of the ball, held it tight in my hot palm, and looked up at the sky; it was beginning to lose its color. I bounced the ball on the pavement once, caught it, tried to read the label that had rubbed off long ago, bounced the ball again. Then I turned and threw it as far as I could, over the asphalt-shingled roof of the house across the street.

My right shoulder and upper arm ached as if they had been near-twisted off by a crazed warehouse goon, but this time I had brought on the pain by myself. I was glad for the sensation, but it didn't help much because it didn't hurt enough.

Vodka was all that I could find in the kitchen cabinet underneath the canister set. I wasn't drinking solo much back then, but I took the bottle of goo with me. Annetta called to me as I was leaving, asked me what was wrong. I told her nothing. I wanted her to believe that I had no stories to tell her about her old friend Albert. And by then she had already given up waiting for me to give her any answers.

I drove the streets, sucking myself sick from the vodka bottle, hating the hot taste, my eyes still dropping tears now and then, my chest still catching a spasm as I remembered some other Bob and Ray routines. The House of Toast was their international chain of restaurants that served only toast. On the Bob and Ray Spelling Bee, one contestant had to spell "interfenestration"; the next contestant got the interrogative, "who."

I drove until it got dark. Then I kept driving. There was a ring around the moon.

"The Gathering Dusk" was a Bob and Ray soap opera about the troubles faced by the elderly Edna Bessinger. In one installment she spent years trapped inside her house by a large snake coiled up outside of her living room window. When she was told that it was just her garden hose, she said that she felt as if a giant weight had been lifted from her shoulders. Did she ever touch a garden hose again?

Bob and Ray had Harry Backstage of the acting Backstages—whose greatest talent as an actor was that he was really good at memorizing things—who once produced a television special called "The Backstages in Africa" which achieved a ratings index of zero. The cast and crew spent the next day trying to decide if that just meant that none of the ratings households had seen the show, or did it mean that no one at all had watched?

Wally Ballou interviewed a cranberry distributer who had never heard of cranberry sauce. The Ben Franklin Look-alike Convention. The Slow Talkers of America.

Kurt Vonnegut once wrote about how sad Bob and Ray both seemed to be when they were off-mike, as if exhausted by being doomed to an existence of making others laugh. The two probably created more funny stuff than anybody in the history of being funny. For year after year, on one radio station or another, they did hour after hour, day after day—almost all of it spontaneous, making-it-up-as-we-go-along kind of stuff. No music, no fill, just two funny guys talking to each other.

Two guys who knew each other so well, effortlessly sharing the same sentence.

I wondered if they were friends. Did they hang around after they got done work? Go out drinking? Did they talk about things with each other, trying to figure them out, trying to figure out how the world worked?

At the end of each show, Ray would say, "Write if you get work." Bob would say, "Hang by your thumbs."

Partners. Productive buddies. If someone assembled Bob and Ray's lifetime achievements, they would fill up the Bob and Ray Overstocked Surplus Warehouse—which also held 322 pair of canvas leggings which were used only once—at the Battle of San Juan Hill—and were used only on the way *up* the hill, not coming back down.

Not much by themselves. Andy Rooney once said that separately they were the dullest guys you'd ever want to talk to. Together, Roy Blount Jr. wrote, they were funnier than anyone else living, including each other. And Vonnegut added that they could go on being funny almost indefinitely.

But I knew even back then that they couldn't. Sooner or later there would be the thought of one of them living in a universe without the other. One friend without the other.

I drove and drank and thought about being upstate years ago, when Albert and I had killed the dog. I had held onto its neck and collar, talking easing words into its ear. Albert put the gun so close to the back of the dog's head that the gun-muzzle was hidden underneath the matted black hair. The dog knew something was coming, it whimpered.

Albert's face had tears resting on it, but the expression seemed detached, disinterested. He told me later, "Sometimes, some things just need a good killing."

Albert knew, and had told me, that sometimes you just have to take care of things. Like with Profumo and Christine Keeler. Yeah. Sometimes you just had to take care of things.

Albert had taken care of things with Arlynn for me. But that left it up to me to take care of things with Albert and what he had done. Could I just leave it buried? Was it too much to just leave alone?

I had once told Albert that a man owes a debt to the world for being allowed to live in it. I owed somebody the debt of the truth and it had to be paid up. I figured I owed this to the world, I owed it to me, I owed it to Arlynn.

Shit, I even owed it to Albert.

At one time I had worked with a very proper and distinguished elderly lady, old New England money type, who would nearly pee her pants every time you reminded her of Mary McGoon's recipe for frozen ginger ale salad, a Bob and Ray routine that she had first heard maybe twenty years earlier.

The Tinkerbell Earth Moving Company, Garish Summit, Einbinder Flypaper, the Monongahela Metal Foundry, which was the world's premier maker of steel ingots. Grub, the Story of Food.

I was so glad that they were that funny. My arm and shoulder still hurt.

I drove through the night and I was still in the exact center of Long Island. When the vodka was gone, I was glad. I pushed the white bottle underneath the driver's seat so that it wouldn't roll around on the floor of the car. I watched the ring around the moon finally fade off.

"Write if you get work."

"Hang by your thumbs."

And so, with the sun finally rising and Mary McGoon's recipe for frozen ginger ale salad bouncing around in my head like a brick inside a clothes-dryer, I walked into the Nassau County detectives' squad room and explained to them over and over again that I knew what had happened to Arlynn Svenson.

❖

February 28, 1970, in The Cave:

"Albert, you never even listened to it like I did. I got the forty-five, I kept playing it. I even ran it on thirty-three a couple times, to check it out, you remember? Listen to the song one time like I did. It was: 'An ugly woman gets your meals on TIME, she'll always give you piece of MIND.'"

"Huh?"

"'An ugly woman gets your meals on TIME, she'll always give you piece of MIND.'"

"No, see? Because, it was because you were too fucking puritanical to hear what was really there. You KNEW what they were saying. Tasti, you KNOW. Just, you're the type guy, sometimes you see and hear things that don't agree with what you think, with how you see the world, so you manage to just don't hear and see them. That's a problem you have. As for me, I'm a realist."

"I know what I heard, Albert, back then. It would be the same thing now, if we went back, got the record. I wish I had the god-damned record right here, I'd play it for you."

"We got no record player."

"On the jukebox."

"JUKE-box? I thought it was JUTE-box."

"JUKE-box."

"What's it, weeping WILLOW or weeping WIDOW?"

"Willow. It's a tree."

"Okay, but what you'd hear—'An ugly woman gets your meals on FAST, she'll always give you a piece of ASS.'"

"No, it wasn't."

"They just had to smear it a little bit, that's all, when they say it, to let the radio play it. Because as long as it's a

156

little bit smeared, the disc jockeys can play it and still claim innocence with a clean conscience. Just to give them an out. They can deny. They knew. Everybody knew what was happening. Just you who didn't. You the only one, you refused to see it."

"Albert, let me remind you, you were the one who thought that Gene Autry was singing 'I'm back in Seattle again.'"

"I did? No, I didn't, that was just a joke, you jerk."

"Back in Seattle again. See, you have a hard time understanding English because you still got all that Hungarian garbage in your head from when you were a little kid. Why would Gene Autry be singing about being in Seattle again? You moron."

"No."

" 'The Girl From Iwo Jima,' huh? And you're the one who thinks the Flamingos, in the back of 'I Only Have Eyes For You', they're chanting, 'Chingachgook.'"

"They are."

"They are. So here's this love ballad, this guy's singing to his girl, and they're chanting the Last of the Mohicans, the name of Natty Bumppo's faithful Indian companion in the background. Why would they be doing that, Albert? Tell me why."

"Who would've guessed, but they are. Just listen. That's what they're saying all right. Ching-ach-gook. Just like 'An ugly woman gets your meals on fast, she'll always give you a piece of ass.' Listen to it, Tasti. I did. Listen and ye shall hear. Oh you of little ears, I applaud you. I appeal to you."

"No, you don't. I KNOW."

"YOU don't know, I know."

"You know?"

"Yeah."

"About what?"

"About this."

"About this?"

157

"Yeah."

"About ugly women?"

"Yeah."

"Albert, YOU know about ugly women?"

"Yeah, do you?"

"About ugly women?"

"Yeah."

"Yeah, Albert, I know, I know about ugly women."

"Fine. Then we both do."

"Okay then."

"Fine."

"Fine."

FOURTEEN

AFTER ANNETTA AND I had been married for a couple months, we had Albert and one of his girlfriends over for dinner at our little newlywed apartment, the top floor of a meter-reader's house. A new-style pool hall had just opened up in Port Washington, with pastel-colored felt pulled tight over the slate and polyester sweaters pulled tight over the waitresses. After dinner Albert and I decided to take the girls out to shoot a couple racks.

A few times during the meal Albert and Annetta had mentioned a name or made reference to a story that I wasn't familiar with, and I had felt a little fillip of jealousy. I knew that Albert had gotten Annetta the job in the warehouse, just like he had done for me, but I didn't know much else about them two together. I tried to remember either one of them telling me specifically about how well they knew each other, or about their friendship, but I couldn't recall. I had never really thought about it before.

I did know that they had first met at a Jets game in Shea Stadium, where Albert's box was adjacent to Annetta's brother's seats, off the thirty yard line. Back then, holding Jets season tickets held no status at all. Just a few years before, when the Jets had been called the Titans and played in the Polo Grounds for Harry Wismer, it was hard *not* to have tickets for a game. You'd go to Food Fair to pick up some bread and sandwich meat and the kid at the check-out would stuff four tickets into your bag when you weren't looking. Or you'd get a bill from Krug's or from the milk man and a couple Titan tickets would be stapled to it with one of those heavy industrial staples that you couldn't pop open with your thumb nail.

Even if you showed up at a game with no tickets at all, the ushers would usually let you in. It was pretty much *laissez faire* back then. The old Boston Patriots had gotten a victory when a guy in an overcoat jumped out of the stands on the last play of the game and knocked down a pass. The refs let it go. Things were pretty casual.

That's how I had thought things between Albert and Annetta had always been—pretty casual—until I was hit that night with something that was so sudden and clear that the nuns would have called it a Beatific Vision.

The four of us—my wife and I, Albert and his date—were at the top of the steps of our apartment, getting ready to go shoot some pool. I watched Albert holding the coat up for my wife to slip her arms into. Annetta with heels was taller than Albert and as her bare arms slipped into the sleeves of her coat, his head tilted forward a bit, toward her, with quiet familiarity. Her face came around toward him; she knew exactly where he would be. As clear as the ice on Leed's Pond.

As hard to miss as if fat Sister Edelina were playing second base in a Little League game, yet I had missed it. Who *was* I, for Christ's sake—Clem Kadiddlehopper?

There's a snapshot of Albert and Annetta together, the two of them. It was taken at Shea Stadium, football season, with a gray-streaked sky behind them. The photograph is darkened with age. A bit of the black center field scoreboard can be seen in one corner. The two of them are seated, squinting, grinning up at the camera lens, Annetta leaning into Albert, who has his arm around her, his hand resting on the shoulder of her dark cloth coat. It's the same coat that he held for her to go shoot pool. No one else is in the picture.

Most of the problems in my life have sprung from somebody hearing what was not said or, more likely, somebody not saying anything when he should have. Me included. Shitty communication puréed with concealment.

Maybe because I spoke about the past all the time, my

wife never talked about it at all. She could sit for hours sipping coffee with me, and she would tell me about the future—her idea of what was to be—right down to the color and nap of the rug we would someday have in the white living room furnished with a white glass-topped table and a white couch and two white chairs.

She seemed to live not in the past, not in the present, but in the future. I realized that I was no one to complain.

Gradually, any discomfort or low-grade anger that I was feeling at the thought of Albert and Annetta's familiarity abated into a powdered residue. It was replaced, maybe foolishly, by some sort of admiration for the both of them. I had looked at what had happened— the fact that I had fallen in love with Albert's lover and she in turn had fallen in love with me. The feelings that they both had for me had silenced everything else in them, as far as anything that they had shared without me.

Albert never showed any indication of frustration, jealousy, or anything else. Ever. Annetta was mine and that was that. Meanwhile Annetta looked forward to a life with me and our future children. So I had nothing to be concerned about.

Whenever Albert and I talked favorite movies, *The Hustler* always got a nod. It wasn't just Paul Newman and Jackie Gleason's cool; it was the idea that something was actually being said underneath the sound of the pool balls clicking together. The way we saw it, the movie taught you that you can't win at anything until you get yourself some character, and the way you get character is by letting life slam you around a little bit and you still survive it. The way Minnesota Fats did when he went in to wash his face after twenty hours of play and came back in, ready to roll some balls. The way Paul Newman did after George C. Scott screws up his girlfriend so bad that she kills herself. Get yourself some character, win the match. "I can't beat you, Fast Eddie."

Albert always beat me at pool, but that night after he had helped Annetta on with her coat, I—like Fast Eddie Felson himself—ran the table on him almost every time.

❖

August 7, 1973, in the courtroom:

"Jay, take the stand."

FIFTEEN

The Trial Preparation

INVESTIGATION, INTERVIEWS, INTERROGATION, arrest, arraignment, hearings, plea entry, trial date, trial preparation. You could click them off like finger-beats from the prosecutor's ring-festooned hands.

Up until that point in my life, I had been lucky enough to avoid getting too close to the grinding wheels of justice, but I had always heard rumors that the grinding went extremely slowly. Assistant D.A. Ron Cloud Carlini's moaning on about aspects of the law tended to support this theory. But overall I had been amazed at how remarkably quickly the wheels had been grinding.

They were certainly grinding much too quickly for me. I wanted to yell out "Fins!" like we used to do in a two-on-two blacktop basketball game. Time-out to tie a sneaker. Five minutes to take a drink from the can of tepid Hi-C lying over there by the logs. A break, to sit and suck in a little air.

But Ron Cloud wouldn't hear of it. He was a man moving forward. He moved around his office from door to window, corner to corner, as he spoke. Every few moments he would turn and look over at me quick—checking me out, making sure I was still tuned in to his words of law.

I was sitting in the prosecutor's small panelled office, counting my teeth with my tongue. Countless endless faculty meetings and college lectures had given me the skill of looking at a speaker as if I were really listening to him. I was doing that for Ron Cloud now, and he seemed satisfied, even pleased.

On some Sundays at Jones Beach, usually in late August or early September, close to hurricane time, the undertow would get so bad that every twenty minutes the lifeguards would be blowing their emergency whistles and heading into the surf to pull somebody out.

We'd be out there body surfing, trying to knock down old ladies who had been driven out from Brooklyn to stand knee deep in the ocean. We'd sputter, "Sorry, lady, accident," and then head back out to do it again.

If the undertow got you, you'd be too embarrassed to call for help, so you'd just ride it as best you could—keep struggling, keep grinning. After a battle, you'd be lucky enough to make it back in, maybe fifty or a hundred yards down the beach from your blanket.

You'd walk back up along the surf line, trying to get back to where you'd started.

That was me right now, caught up in the legal undertow, being dragged, near powerless, just trying to survive and get back to the beach. Back to my buddies on the towel.

Not too many months ago, I had lain sweating in bed, trying to figure out what had happened to Arlynn Svenson. Albert wouldn't help me out, nobody else knew anything, so I had been left trying to figure things out for myself.

Now I had to do that again. But this time I had help. First from the cops, then prosecutors, then their investigators, then with the prosecutors again.

Together we saw this: Arlynn's home alone, watching her soap operas, she lets Big Daddy Pimp Albert come in. She's scared, but craving adventure; he's preoccupied, thinking, "Just get this done." My name doesn't come up at all.

Albert's the whoremonger—Casanova by way of Tony Curtis—and she's Lolita. Her father's gone, out boozing.

She starts coming on to this guy—a hiked-up leg, lipping a cigarette, some screwed-up faux-sexy lines from some old movie. Teenage breasts underneath a sweatshirt. She's not even considering asking him why he's here.

Albert's thinking—just do a quick favor for a friend, then it's back to the warehouse. This girl's bait. Still though . . .

Still though, a lay's a lay, you take what you can get. This kid's sort of creepy, she's dressed like a slob, but she's blessed with a body that could stop a taxi cab at forty yards.

"Who you live here with?"

"My father."

"Where's he?"

"Now?"

"Where's your father now?"

"I don't know. Out drunk."

"When's he coming back?"

"I don't know. When he's drunk, a couple days sometimes."

"Couple days. Wow."

So Albert lets it play out. He forgets his troubles for a half hour. "Hallelujah, c'mon, get happy."

He dips it.

For her, it's a day to remember, to put on her calendar, write about in her diary—if she kept one. A day to tell her friends about—if she had any. For Albert, it's a quick piece before supper. Certainly nothing special.

Afterwards, Arlynn's dreamy-eyed, trying to smoke in bed without burning the place down. She puts a tape into the cassette player beside her bed.

Albert starts pulling on his socks; he asks her if there's anything to eat. An ugly woman gets your meals on fast, she'll always give you a piece of ass.

Out at the kitchen table, music still coming from the bedroom, Albert's eating eggs, they're broken and blackened around the edges. Finally, he starts sliding into his strong-arm talk. "Arlynn, we gotta talk. I really like you a lot. I like the time we've had here together. It was stunning. I like you, but I gotta tell you, there's some people, you're really getting these people mad at you, with some stuff you been saying. And these are not good people to have mad at you. Because when they get mad, then they get scared too. When people get mad, and scared, they and their friends, they react poorly. Often they do. It could be dangerous."

Arlynn's a little pissed off about having to cook the eggs. She's listening for her father's car to drive up in the driveway. She has no idea what this guy is telling her about—scared, mad people. All she knows is, she's being threatened by the guy that she just took to bed. She doesn't care to be treated like that.

Eventually she tells him to fuck off—first time she's ever said that to anybody for real—but what the hell, she's been made a woman now. She likes the feel of the curse word on her tongue, the feel of it coming out. She says it to him a couple more times.

The guy reacts poorly. A glaze comes over his eyes. He starts up and at her. She goes into one of her fits, like in the principal's office when they were trying to get her to go home that time. Now, for Albert, she's screaming, crying, kicking furniture, maybe even taking a swipe at him.

But here's the thing. Albert knows how to deal with hysterical whores, any age. He's seen it a thousand times, with his girls. He grabs an arm, maybe twists the skin a little, maybe a quick open-handed slap. Just to get her attention. Just to get her calmed down.

Drags her back to the bedroom, the kitchen's too wide open.

But this little slut doesn't get calm. Instead she goes nuts. She comes at him—cat claws and teeth. She's not just hooping around with this guy; this is for real. He ain't no pansy-assed high school principal, but she ain't no pansy-assed school girl either. She's a woman been wronged.

Albert's trying to hold onto her wrists, trying to reach into his pocket for some bills. He gets them out, slaps a hundred on the table, but the sight of money just gets her crazier. Her screams are louder, there's somebody's blood on Albert's shirt, on the white sheets, on this crazy girl's face. She's still going for Albert's eyes.

Albert's trying to check windows for the neighbors. He's got this kid going nuts in a first floor bedroom of a little cape in crowded-together Levittown. At least the blinds are closed.

He tries to grab her arm again, then to take her face into his hand, between his thumb and his strong fingers. She's too quick, moving too wild for him to grab her.

Albert's thinking: Number one, neighbors; two, the father coming home; three, pissed-off crazy girl who likes to tell people that older men sexed her; four, trying to help my buddy Tasti, got to get this little tramp to shut up; five, those God-damned Yacovazzi Brothers, trying to steal my business, they're driving me nuts.

His intent—maybe just to silence her, maybe to punish her, maybe to kill her.

The deed—a skull-crushing impact at the corner of the skull above the left eye, intersecting the hairline.

He wraps her in the white, embroidered bedspread that has tassels on four sides. He takes the candleholder, or whatever it was he used to club her, out of the house with him. As he lugs her out the back door, Herman's Hermits are still singing the soundtrack back in the bedroom.

"Is that it, Albert? Is that what happened to Arlynn? What, Albert? What?"

"That's what happened . . . if that's what you want."

Ron Cloud Carlini was going over the story with me— "as our office sees it, Jay, as we speculate on the way things happened"—for maybe the fifteenth time. I was losing interest and respect at about an equal rate.

I sat there. I ran my tongue across the inside of my teeth, clicking off a number at each space. Seven to the front center tooth, seven more on the other side. Total top teeth—fourteen. I'd had my wisdoms taken out back when I was in college. Same count on the bottom, although sometimes it came up short because the bottom incisors were lined up so well that it was tough for the tongue to tell them apart. Tooth count for the entire mouth—twenty-eight. Yup, it all totaled up okay.

Ron Cloud kept talking. I tried to read the names of the books on his shelves. I counted my teeth with my tongue again, but I lost count when he asked me a question that I was supposed to answer. He turned to the office window and started talking again. I started the tooth count again. Twenty-eight.

As he was looking out at the traffic on Old Country Road, I was checking out his clothes. His suit was a smooth three-piece, somewhere between green, gray and yellow. Shirt cuffs sharp enough to cut steak. His shoes looked like the usual wing-tips up top, but they had thick yellow sponge for the soles and heels. Albert and I used to call that beefsteak grizzle. We'd say, "Hey, man, you're wearing your beefsteak shoes. You go in snow or we pay the tow."

When Ron Cloud got done with his monotone briefing, he sat back down into red leather upholstery and he asked me if I had any questions of him.

"Just one," I told him. I pointed to his feet. "What'd you call those shoes, anyway?"

Nassau County got to try the case even though Arlynn's body was discovered by an illegal rabbit hunter up in Orange County. *Newsday* said it was because a tandem investigation by both counties' district attorneys, assisted by the state police and the F.B.I., had ascertained that the crime had been committed on Long Island.

In reality, it was simply a case of Nassau having a bigger political fist. Nassau wanted the case. Some of the cops and D.A.'s downstate had disliked Albert for years, from even before he beat the rap on the truckload of stolen plastic baby-wind-up crib mobiles.

Some of these guys looked upon Albert as a red-shit stylist. There were so few things about their jobs that kept them coming to the office each morning. Nailing a stylist like Albert Niklozak would be one of them.

Their press leaks were always careful to include the nickname "Nickels," almost as a Christian middle name for Albert, although neither I nor any of his friends could ever remember actually calling him that.

There were dual charges—murder second degree as the main call and manslaughter as the safety net.

An upstate medical examiner had ascertained just what the District Attorney's office had wanted him to. Reports with words like "bludgeoned," and vague time frames, and scientific references to the body of what had been an unscientific young girl. And a crushing impact to the head, at the corner of the skull above the left eye, intersecting the hairline.

For a few days after I had first come in to the cops, the D.A.'s office had kept me shaking with threats to charge me as an accessory in the crime. They kept pointing out that it was I who had set the "deadly chain of events in progress." They really talked like that.

But somebody must have made a closed-door strategy decision then, because suddenly I was the golden boy of the office. By the time the coffee had cooled in the porcelain cup that they had handed me—sugar, no cream, the way I like it—I had figured out that the trial was going to be a contest of my image against Albert's. I was to be the soft-speaking English teacher, at first harassed by a lovesick, imbalanced teenager, then tortured by an insane act committed by an out-of-control low-life acquaintance who was left over from my childhood.

I was a family man, Albert was a pimp. I graded student papers at home as my wife made me tea. Albert robbed trucks and beat hundred-pound teenagers to death. I went to parent conferences; Albert dumped bodies.

That's how they planned to play it in court. Same thing in the newspapers.

The prosecutor named to the case was so ambitious that he kept his head and eyes angled up toward the ceiling and the sky, as if he were checking out the spot where he would be in a few years. Ron Cloud Carlini. He was half American Indian, half third-generation Italian, back before either was fashionable. If he had two more halves, they would have been elephant and bull terrier, because the guy never forgot and he never unclenched his jaw.

He had been the assistant D.A. who had prosecuted Albert for the truckload of stolen baby wind-up mobiles. When Albert had been found not guilty, he had grinned and given Ron Cloud a gift-wrapped mobile, like the ones in evidence. Ron Cloud's associates had probably agreed that this alone was cause enough to let him have the opportunity to castrate Albert this time out.

Ron Cloud had an investigator and an assistant working with him full-time for this case, but he personally took charge of every phase of the trial preparation.

Someone once told me that in all of government—local, municipal, state, federal—the one person who has the most power to do you harm is the prosecutor. Most people agree with that. All the prosecutors certainly do.

The trial date got closer. Ron Cloud had me in his office again, this time for almost two hours, lecturing me on nothing but my court demeanor. This didn't even concern my testimony, it was just the general appearance stuff. He would work with me on specific testimony and my on-stand performance on the evening before I would testify.

For now he was just molding my in-court image for me—when I should be there, where I should sit, how I should dress, who should be with me. Crap-like stuff like that. Two hours worth.

Showing me how to be Joe Louis to Albert's Max Schmelling. Wally Cleaver and Eddie Haskell.

Albert's lawyer was Lupo, the same one who had defended him on the wind-up plastic mobiles. Ron Cloud told me that he respected Lupo as an adversary, but he let contempt creep into his voice as he said it. Ron Cloud told me that we would have another briefing right before Lupo cross-examined me.

Albert had introduced me to Lupo once, at the party after the mobile trial. They were both holding champagne. Albert had called him "Loop Hole," and Lupo had laughed himself into tears.

A couple nights before the trial, a Mets game was on at the apartment and I was trying to get interested in it when the doorbell rang. Annetta led Bobby Gallaga into the room. He asked Annetta to excuse us. After she had gone to sit with James Albert, Gallaga pulled his chair up close to the recliner where I was sitting. He looked at me with what he apparently thought would pass for earnestness.

Since he had begun attempting to get into politics, Bobby had tried to change his appearance. What was left of his wispy blond hair was neatly combed across the top of his head. He wore a blazer, gray slacks, and saddle shoes.

I told him, "Nice shoes, Bobby. Tell me this, can you wear them to bowl in?"

He said to me, "Jay, listen, Albert wants you to go see him."

Albert was temporarily out on bail.

I asked Bobby, "You just came from him? He sent you here?"

Bobby said, "That part doesn't matter. That's neither here nor there."

"Where is it?"

"What?"

"Bobby, I can't. I can't do that."

"Why not?"

"Listen, Skull, I just can't, that's all. It's a legal thing. It would mess up the trial. For *both* sides, I mean, of course. The lawyers wouldn't like it."

"For Christ sake, Jay, forget the lawyers. The guy's your friend, he's just asking you to go meet with him over there. Go see him. He's your friend, for Christ sake."

"Bobby, he killed somebody. He killed a seventeen-year-old girl."

Bobby said, "We don't know that. We don't know that for sure."

I told him, "Yes, we do."

Bobby just shrugged his shoulders, New York style, and looked down at his saddle shoes. He didn't say anything for awhile. Then he got up and said, "Jay, I can't tell you who sent me, or who I'm affiliated with. There's legal concerns, as you yourself pointed out. Out of respect for the human condition, it'd be best this were kept a clandestine meeting. Do you know what that means?"

"Bobby, I'm an English teacher."

"Very good. Very good." As he went to leave, he told me that our society needs more teachers. "So you just forget I was here, okay?"

"Of course," I told him. I was walking him over to the door. "I always do that."

Right before the door closed, Bobby Gallaga said to me, "Albert says you should remember what he told you. The advice, right before we tried to pull Cookie's house down with a train."

I knew what Albert was asking me to do. He knew I remembered all that stuff with Buster Cook, the stuff we had said to each other. I remember things like that. Albert was telling me to stuff a rag, to keep my damned mouth shut. About everything.

The day after Bobby Gallaga came by the apartment, I called up Ron Cloud Carlini and begged him to let me go see Albert.

Ron Cloud listened, then he spoke to me slowly, like you would to a child. He explained about mistrials, about witness tampering, improper judicial conduct. He said to me, "Jay, you go talk to Albert and they've got a perfect appeal if they lose. Why do you want to talk to him anyway? What good is it going to do?"

I said, "None, I guess," and I hung up.

It had taken me three hours to get through to Ron Cloud, to beg him to let me speak to Albert. But the truth was, I didn't want to speak to Albert at all. I hadn't gone to see him before I went to the cops, and I didn't want to go see him now. Truth was—I had called up Ron Cloud just to have him talk me out of something that I wasn't going to do anyway.

Two days before the trial was scheduled to start, I came as close as I ever would to hitting Annetta. Instead, I just put my fist through sheetrock in our bedroom. Later I went to sleep wondering how Albert had treated her, back when they had been together.

On the day before the trial, I walked unannounced into Ron Cloud Carlini's office and told him that I was not going to testify. "Do what you want to me, Ron Cloud, I don't care, I'm sorry. No deal."

He looked up from the little note pad on his desk, he smiled, got up and closed the door to the outer office. He asked me to sit down.

In a clear and steady voice, he enumerated the charges that his office could bring against me if he wished. He tapped the pencil on the polished wood top of his desk. One tap per charge. I didn't hear all of the charges he listed, but there was obstruction of justice, there was false testimony, there was accessory, conspiracy to commit murder.

When he was finished, he didn't even ask me for a reply. He just got up, put a firm palm into the small of my back, and shoveled me out of the room. "See you tomorrow. Remember to wear a quiet suit jacket and a tie."

The Prosecution

Ron Cloud Carlini could move around a courtroom like he had Fernando Lamas's head and body on Donald O'Connor's feet. The trial judge, a faggy-looking little guy named Kmetz, watched Ron Cloud like he wanted to date him. Each time the judge whispered to the bailiff during the trial, I figured they were talking about how hot and sexy Ron Cloud was looking today.

One time the judge had a note delivered to Ron Cloud's table. I figured it read, "Do you like me? Yes. No. Check one." I'd seen this trick a lot when I had to do a junior high study hall.

In contrast to Ron Cloud Carlini, Lupo, over on the defense table, looked like the Pillsbury Dough Boy, but without the doughboy's macho demeanor.

I had never been in a courtroom before, and had based my expectations on the movies. I pictured either a hot little sweaty band-box full of guys wearing garters on their shirt sleeves, like in *To Kill a Mockingbird*, or else giant rising windows with teak and ebony frames, like in *Purple Heart*.

Courtroom 7-B in Mineola was white, windowless, barely big enough for a half-court game of basketball. The room reminded me of a doctor's waiting room with the ceiling raised up a couple feet.

The acoustics were lousy and when I didn't lean forward, I missed every third or fourth word that anybody said. Except for the words of Ron Cloud, which bounced around the walls like bullets ricocheting off rocks.

In the opening statement, Ron Cloud's assistant told the jury that they would establish motive, means, and opportunity for the crime. The motive, I knew, would be centered on *my* testimony, explaining to the jury that our friendship and my request for help was the original reason that the alleged murderer headed on over to the victim's house, to shut her up. Means would be the blow to the head; the murder weapon remaining undiscovered after such a long time. The opportunity was certainly there—a suburban cape, at the time of the crime holding only the assailant and the victim, the victim's father being absent.

The prosecution would try to get as much of Albert's past as possible into testimony. His temper, his past brushes with violence, especially against women, his loose affiliation with organized crime, that would all be fair game as far as the prosecution was concerned.

Lupo, naturally, would try to deflect as many of these points as possible. Judge Kmetz would spend a lot of trial time dreaming about Ron Cloud's ass and ruling on whether his points were admissible or not.

Albert sat motionless at the defense table, drinking water, sometimes holding two fingers and a thumb up to his mouth, almost never looking my way.

The first two witnesses just covered the grisly identification of Arlynn Svenson's body. She'd been wearing a high school ring and her gold anklet with the letter *A*.

Before I started teaching school, I used to love to read certain books over and over. The habit had started in high school, when I had read, then reread and reread, Mickey Spillane's *The Girl Hunters*. The first line in it is, "They found me in the gutter."

Then teaching English had forced me to reread certain books many times as part of the work, every year—plays like *Death of a Salesman* and *The Glass Menagerie*, novels like *Gatsby*. Even though I loved them, it left me less committed to rereading non-school stuff.

And so eventually I found myself only rereading two

works of literature. The first was a tiny volume called *Wodehouse at War*. I considered P. G. Wodehouse to be the best of all writers—not just the funniest, but the best. A rumor had spread that accused him of collaborating with the Nazis during World War II. The book cleared up the story, got to the truth, completely exonerated him. Each time I finished reading it, I was left with a good, clean feeling, like the one I'd get after dropping off a load of garbage at the dump.

The other work that I read constantly was supplied to me by Ron Cloud Carlini. It was the transcript of the Albert J. Niklozak murder trial, State of New York, County of Nassau, Docket Number H14-8-1973.

Q: And how long, in your estimation, had the body been dead by the time it was discovered?

A: Our best estimates, only be estimates, would be a year, give or take two or three months.

Q: We realize how difficult such an estimation must be to make. But a year, give or take a few months. Body was discovered April of this year. That could, let's see, place the time of death, possibly at least, at last June, June of last year. Correct?

A: Yes, possible. Possibly.

Q: Naturally, it's not your place, the place of your office, to equate that with June 22, the day and date of the victim's disappearance, is it?

A: No, that's something to be taken into consideration by the investigators. We're just doing the lab work. Straight science.

Q: The, uh, were you able to determine the cause of death?

A: Difficult, with the long time between the death and our examination. If I had to make a determination, I would say, there was a cranial indentation, you see, quite extensive, we found. So I would have to say, if I had to make a determination, cause of death was an impact at the corner of the skull above the left eye, intersecting the hairline.

Q: And the blood spots raised in the trunk of the accused's car, they were, how old?

A: Over a few months. It's hard to tell beyond that.

Q: Could be ten months, the range of time between the alleged murder and the discovery of the body?

A: That's entirely possible.

Q: Likely?

A: Likely as any.

Q: And these spots, these spots of blood, completely consistent with the blood of the victim?

A: AB Positive, yes.

Q: Realizing, of course, that blood work is an imprecise science, still, the facts remains, could very possibly be the blood of the victim?

A: Yes.

Q: More importantly, in fact, very, very much more importantly, tell us about the hair strands found in the accused's car trunk, would you, Doctor?

A: They were strands of hair from the head of the deceased.

Q: No doubt? Arlynn Svenson's hair?

A: Virtually none. There existed a statistical certainty that the hairs were the same, from the same individual.

Q: Couldn't be similar hair? Hair from a person with the same hair color? Texture? Things like that?

A: No, very most likely not. The hair was the same. From the same person.

Q: And you've been living there on Acorn Street for how long?

A: Twenty years, a little more.

Q: And you saw the defendant—that's Mr. Niklozak

over there— you saw him enter the Svenson's house, didn't you?

Q: Yes.
A: Never saw him leave.
Q: No.
Q: Never saw Arlynn Svenson alive again?
Q: No.

Q: Miss Reno, could you tell the court then, what Mr. Niklozak did?
A: He hit me.
Mr. Lupo. Objection, Your Honor, Councilor is way off base here.
Mr. Carlini. I'm just trying to establish some frames of mind here, Your Honor. The personalities involved here are tantamount to the case.
The Court. I'll let that stand. Proceed on please, Councilor.
Mr. Carlini. Thank you, sir.

Continued Direct Examination by Mr. Carlini

Q: Miss Reno then, you told the court that Mr. Niklozak hit you?
A: Yes.
Q: That would be an open-handed slap, like you might give a recalcitrant child?
A: That would be a punch, a fist punch, sir, to my forehead. Knocked me down.
Q: There was a certain amount of damage done, to yourself?
A: Yeah. Yes. The damage done was a welt, a black-and-blue for days. I used make-up on it. I had to. So I could go to work. And it was headaches for a long time too. I don't remember how long. But it had hurt my neck too, it was so strong. So I got headaches too from it.
Q: And on this specific occasion, for this specific offense, Mr. Niklozak was arrested and charged with?

Mr. Lupo: Objection, Your Honor.
Mr. Carlini: Withdrawn then.

Arlynn's father was called to the stand. Ron Cloud made sure everybody knew that the old guy was dying of cancer. His sunken and shapeless face, his bird-like eyes, chicken-boned neck and jaw, and prominent Adam's apple, all made him look more like an Oklahoma shit-bird than a Long Island chiropractor.

Ron Cloud began the questioning by painting a picture of the father-daughter relationship—emphasizing how hard it was to be a single parent, especially the father of a daughter. Lupo couldn't object to the line of questioning without looking like slime and risking alienating the jury. The testimony went very slowly, about twenty minutes worth of this mode.

Then, so slowly that no one really noticed it, Ron Cloud nudged things into the area of Arlynn's troubles, her quirks. For awhile it just sounded like a sympathy ploy for the victim, but after awhile everyone began seeing a picture of a very troubled girl, one that could drive persons coming in contact with her to distraction, to aggravation, maybe to violence.

Q: She would never back down then, calm herself and back down, once she was upset?

A: No, she couldn't. She'd be not capable. You'd just have to go, leave her alone for awhile, let her cool down herself.

Q: And if you didn't?

A: If you?

Q: If you kept the, the pressure on her? Kept at her even if she was aggravated?

A: She'd blow up. She'd get very active, violent, she'd go after you.

Q: After you?

A: Out of control. Trying to hurt someone.

Q: Did Arlynn ever hurt you, Mr. Svenson?

A: Yes. Just scratches sometimes. A bite. That was when she was younger. I learned to deal with it. How to avoid that.

Q: And that was by avoiding her, getting away from the scene.

A: Right. Leave her lie.

Q: But, many of us are parents, we understand, did you ever, Mr. Svenson, find yourself losing control with her? Getting angry?

A: Sure.

Q: Did you ever find yourself just holding yourself back, restraining yourself from hitting her?

A: I never hit her, hurt her.

Q: No, I know, I'm sure. I guess what I'm trying to ask is, if you, if her father had to use all his will power to stop from striking this very, let's say, frustrating child, then, someone, else, who didn't know her, had no feeling for her, might have an even more difficult time. Restraining himself.

A: Sure. I suppose.

Q: And if that person had a history of violent behavior toward women.

Mr. Lupo: Objection, Your honor.

The Court: That's sustained.

Continued Direct Examination by Mr. Carlini

Q: Well then, let's go the other way. Mr. Svenson, the court might be thinking, the jury might be saying, sure that's how a teenage girl, a troubled one, would act with a family member, with her father, but that would never happen with someone outside the family. Could it?

A: You mean getting wild?

Q: Yes. Losing control of herself.

A: The school used to call. She'd get like that with the teachers and things. She'd be sent home a few days. Suspended.

Q: And, once at home, you'd know enough to stay away from her, let her be, instead of exerting any pressure.

A: Yeah.

Q: Pressure that would cause her to act aggressively again.

A: Yeah.

Q: But you never hurt your daughter, hit your daughter, Mr. Svenson.

A: Never. Spanked her maybe, as a child, like all parents do.

Q: But never found yourself losing control and going after her.

A: No.

Q: Because, again, you knew how she should be dealt with.

A: Sure.

Q: But now, again, you had to be happy that some other adult, at the school, of course, they're trained how to deal with children who have lost control over themselves. But you had to be relieved, weren't you, that in other aspects of her life, that she didn't come in contact with someone who didn't know or care, didn't know how she ticked, or let's say, someone who was used to meeting violence with violence, confrontation with confrontation, if someone like this were to ever come in contact with your daughter.

Mr. Lupo: Oh, wow, objection, Your Honor. Haven't we been here already?

Arlynn's father testified that he had left the house that June day, leaving Arlynn in pretty good spirits. She was about to graduate from high school. She was looking forward to beginning life as an adult.

Mr. Svenson had left the house feeling pretty good about how things were turning out for his tiny family. He had left then feeling like a successful parent, but had returned to never see his troubled little girl again.

The witness chair in Courtroom 7-B was made out of wood, but it felt like a two-inch deep plastic pool of warm slime as I pushed my ass down into it. I never looked at Albert the whole time I was up, but I knew that he was watching me.

I had monitored cafeteria study halls of seventy kids, seventh period, all by myself. I had waited in a doctor's office to get test results on my wife and my unborn child. But in my entire life, time never went as slowly for me as it did on that stand.

Q: How long?

A: Long time. We met, back in grammar school, maybe fourth grade.

Q: So you know the defendant well?

A: Yes, I did. As well as anyone in the world.

Q: Knew his strong points, his weak points, of his character?

A: Uh-huh.

Q: Speak up.

A: Yes, I did. I knew him, his character.

Q: Let's skip ahead a number of years. What was your thought, that first day after, when Arlynn Svenson was gone from school, that first day after you had asked Mr. Niklozak to talk to her for you?

A: I got nervous.

Q: That?

A: That something had happened to her.

Mr. Lupo: Object. This is supposition.

Mr. Carlini: Not at all, your honor. I'm asking Mr. Tasti what he was thinking. Nobody knows better than him.

The Court: Overruled.

Continued Direct Examination by Mr. Carlini

Q: Your belief was that Mr. Niklozak, no, that something had gone horribly wrong with your plan to have Mr. Niklozak speak to Arlynn?

A: It occurred to me.

Q: And a year after that, when it was brought to your attention that the decomposed body of Arlynn Svenson had been discovered buried, up in Newburgh.

A: What?

Q: Your first suspicion was?

A: I thought that Albert might be somehow involved.

Q: Somehow involved? Wasn't it a bit more than that? Isn't it true that you immediately went to the police and reported that you felt that you knew what had happened, thus kicking off the investigation that has led to this trial?

A: Yeah, pretty quick after that, I did.

Whenever I tried to detour slightly off the course Ron Cloud told me that we'd be taking, he grabbed the steering wheel and yanked us both back on. I was outclassed and overpowered.

Even Lupo seemed to be going along for the ride that Ron Cloud was taking us all on.

Q: And finally now, let me ask you, how do you feel about Mr. Niklozak now, Jay?

A: I pity him. I don't understand him.

Q: Anything else?

A: I love him.

So it was a matter of public record.

In the cross-exam, Lupo tried his best to dirty me however he could, as the jury's eyes went from me sitting upright on the stand to Albert slouching at the table.

Q: My client didn't know Miss Svenson.

A: No, not until he went over there.

Q: You knew her quite well.

A: She'd been a student of mine.

Q: Well, it was a bit more than that, huh? You've already given us testimony that she made very strong sexual advances toward you.

A: Right.

Q: She offered to be your lover.

A: Right.

Q: But you, of course, declined.

A: Strongly.

Q: Now, Mr. Niklozak sitting over there, as far as you know, was never offered the, um, sexual opportunity that was offered to you by the young lady.

A: I don't know.

Q: You have no reason to believe he was.

A: No, I guess not.

Q: Just you.

But it really didn't matter what Lupo asked me or how I answered him. All the jury had to do was to look from me to Albert, from my performance to his, then back again. I wasn't the type to scare, deceive, or intimidate anybody.

The Defense

At court recess, one of Ron Cloud's law clerks told me that Lupo was a mafia-quality lawyer. That could have been true, but I knew that it was Albert himself who had sketched out and welded together the frame of his defense. It was deny and then shut up. It was the same strategy he had told me to use way back when we decided to yank Buster Cook's house down with a train. To Albert, it would have worked then and it would work now.

Just deny, then deny you denied it. Then clamp your gums together for good.

Q: Albert, let's start off with the only question there is, really. Did you kill Arlynn Svenson?

A: No.

Q: You and I have both sat here listening to the days of prosecution testimony. I didn't hear, maybe I missed something, did you ever hear a reason for you to kill Arlynn Svenson?

The Court: Counselor, just ask your questions please. Save the soapbox till later.

Continued Direct Examination by Mr. Lupo

Q: Sorry, your honor. Albert, let me simplify it. Did you have any reason whatsoever to kill Arlynn Svenson?

A: No.

Q: You went over there to talk to her, because your friend, Jay Tasti, had asked you to.

A: Right.

Q: Just to talk to her. And, and what happened when you went over there?

A: We talked a little bit. Little bit. I told her what a nice guy Tasti was. I explained to her how upset he was getting. I asked her to treat him okay, don't try to mess him up. She told me, fine.

Q: She never began violently attacking you, scratching, kicking, going crazy, as we've heard here in testimony?

A: Nah, nothing like that.

Q: She'd have no reason to.

A: Nope.

Q: And when you left her?

A: She was fine.

Q: Albert, we've heard over and over again from the prosecution witnesses that Arlynn was ready to get on with her life beyond high school. You agree with that, don't you?

A: Sure.

Q: She actually spoke about leaving town, traveling, relocating to another part of the country. You two spoke about that.

A: Yeah, we did.

Q: Just as her father, and I believe even your friend Mr. Tasti, have testified about her.

A: Right.

Q: And you believe, that's what she did.

A: Yeah, for awhile.

Q: Albert, though, then how do you account for the year-old blood and hair fibers in the trunk of your car?

A: Well, thinking about that, the only thing I can come up with, the only time blood and hair's been in there, I've carried deer in there, from hunting.

Q: And you've lent your car out, to friends, various friends, various times, and they could have put something in there that left things.

A: I guess so.

Q: But your best bet is, the deer.

A: Yeah, well, that's all I can think of.

Q: You've never transported a human body in that trunk, have you?

A: No.

Q: So, if I were to tell you that the so-called science of hair, blood and tissue identification has made flagrant, egregious errors in the past, at times even mistaking human hair for non, you wouldn't be surprised, would you?

A: Not at all.

Mr. Carlini: Your Honor, are we listening to some sort of science symposium now?

The prosecution's cross examination on Albert. Ron Cloud was chomping to go after him, but whenever he asked me about Albert, I told him that the guy would never let you score on him up there on the witness stand. Albert would slouch and give one-word answers and deny, deny,

deny. Ron Cloud grinned at me as if to say, "You don't know what I can do to a witness, when I want to."

But he must have been listening to what I was telling him, because Ron Cloud let his assistant handle the cross. Ron Cloud looked like he wasn't even watching.

Q: You own a camp upstate New York, don't you, Mr. Niklozak?

A: No.

Q: No, you don't? A camp? A hunting cabin? A little place up in Newburgh, you don't?

A: Someone in my family owns a place up there. I don't, though.

Q: But you frequent it?

A: I been known to.

Q: Big area up there, isn't it? I mean the Adirondack region itself. Square miles upon miles. Bigger than some entire states, isn't it?

A: Big.

Q: Tell us, to the best of your knowledge, how far your family's hunting camp is from the site where we found the body of Arlynn Svenson buried.

A: I don't know, because I don't know where it was, you found the body of Arlynn Svenson buried.

The prosection had to give the jury a little bit of a show, so they popped Albert with a few references to the blood, the hair, his temper, his past, even called him "Nickels" once. But basically they just let it go.

Ron Cloud was more interested in winning the case than in getting his cookies off in front of a jury.

Q: Mr. Niklozak, would you do anything for a friend?

A: Just about.

The last defense witness was June Copley, a guidance counselor at the high school.

Q: So, in addition to your work in the guidance office, you've taken a number of psychology credits?

A: Yes, many.

Q: You are very close to being recognized by the State of New York as a practicing psychologist.

A: As close as you could be.

Q: This, coupled with your years of dealing with students at your high school, often troubled, often, I don't know, hurt, all this has made you quite an expert in dealing with kids like this.

A: Yes, I'd say so.

Q: So, Miss, you prefer Ms., Ms. Copley, tell us, we've heard again and again that Arlynn Svenson was anxious to graduate from school and to get off Long Island and to live in another part of the country. Is that true?

A: Yes, she was not happy in her present living.

Q: And she did graduate?

A: Yes.

Q: So. Perfect time to leave home?

A: For her, she felt.

Q: Her clothes were gone, when her dad got home. Some personal possessions. This then, is the pattern of a young woman leaving, isn't it?

A: I suppose so.

Q: But now, here's a problem, she never told her father. No good- byes. Does that strike you as strange, Ms.?

A: Not too. Arlynn often mentioned her having a very strained relationship with her father. She kept, I believe, as much as she could from him.

Q: You would have predicted that when she left, she would not announce it to him?

A: I wouldn't be surprised.

Q: And since she was close to no one else, being what she was, a strange, secretive, isolated, young lady, she'd very likely just take her things and head on out. *Au revoir.*

A: I suppose so.

Q: But, as we adults know, we can't run from our problems, can we, Ms. Copley. So. Wouldn't you say that the flaws that you saw in the young lady's personality, could have, especially, being a young woman, on the road, alone, attractive, sexually interested, sometimes inciting violence in others, the prosecution has told us, isn't there a very good chance that such an easy target, an easy prey, could have fallen into a dangerous, even murderous, situation while out there on the road?

A: With Arlynn, it certainly could have happened.

Q: This case is a tragedy, we all agree on that. One of the most tragic aspects, of course, is that the body lay buried for almost a year before discovery. In that time, here's my question to you, in that time, decomposition made it impossible to tell if the girl had been sexually assaulted, but she could very well have been. And that, considering what you know about Arlynn and her personality, that would not have surprised you in the least, would it have, Miss Copley?

A: No.

Q: Sexually attacked by some predator, on the road, her being completely defenseless, him striking her on the head, raping her, killing her, burying her. And us down here in her home area, trying to bring this crime back home. We might be way, way off-target here, mightn't we, Ms. Copley?

As the court was ready for the defense's closing statement, Judge Kmetz ended the session for the day. It was then that a strange thing happened. As they were leading Albert away, the procession of guards and lawyers and prisoner somehow veered toward me. I was sitting by myself in the gallery.

Shackled and manacled, Albert shuffled up to me, then stopped, looked at me awhile and said quietly but very clearly, "Jay, take the stand."

That was a strange thing for him to say for a number of reasons. I had already testified days before. Albert couldn't want any more of that. Also, in our two lifetimes together, he had never called me anything but Tasti. Until now.

Worst of all, Albert's face suddenly had a complete crushing sadness to it as he spoke to me. It seemed to be registering feelings way out there beyond the depression of what was happening to him on that particular day. Then I realized that it wasn't a sadness that was meant for *him*, it was a sadness meant for *me*. The only time I could remember Albert's face looking like that was when we were dragging the Shadow down a muddy slope on our way to put a bullet into his brain. Before the mask of resignation had replaced the look on Albert's face.

The temperature was in the high eighties that night in my apartment. I lay in bed with the windows locked.

The Verdict and Aftermath

After the judge had read the verdict to the courtroom, Lupo asked that each member of the jury be audibly polled. A court guard said that he had never heard the word "Guilty" pronounced so confidently and peacefully, twelve times in a row.

Albert pursed his lips, looked over at his lawyer, then nodded to the jury, as if to tell them, "Hey, what could you expect?"

Very often in a court trial, the lawyers and judge gain, everybody else loses. That's what happened in the Albert Niklozak murder trial.

The trial judge soon after became New York State

Supreme Court Judge David M. Kmetz, taking the place of a magistrate who had gone nuts and been found trying to board the Staten Island Ferry wearing just a jock strap and a fireman's helmet.

Ron Cloud Carlini used the publicity of the trial to help him run for the top county D.A. slot in Nassau, which is what he was after all along. Once ensconced there, he got himself season tickets to the Knickerbockers at the Garden, just a few rows off court-side. You could pick him out sometimes on televised games. Someone said he had Rangers tickets too.

On the day of Albert's sentencing, Ron Cloud gave him the same gift-wrapped baby mobile that Albert had given to Ron Cloud a few years before. The card with it read, "He who laughs last."

Albert said to him, "Hey, that's original."

When Albert couldn't pay his legal bills, Lupo took a share of the warehouse, along with the Yacovazzi brothers, and they all made some good money selling off all the non-inventoried stock.

Albert got twenty years, eligible for parole after the first ten. This time, as they led him out of the courtroom by me, he didn't look up or say anything. I tried to picture him ten years older. It would be ten rock-hard years, so how much worse would that make it?

I reminded myself that I'd be ten years closer to death too by then. And I knew my years wouldn't be much easier than Albert's. That helped a little.

One week after he had been sent away, I got an envelope from the Clinton Correctional Facility at Dannemora, New York. Inside was a small folded note that read, "Tasti—I'm waiting. I'm waiting." It was signed "Albert."

I wrote him back a letter that went five pages. It took me most of a morning to write. Finally, I reread it, went into the kitchen, and threw the pages into the flip-top kitchen garbage can.

Instead of the letter, I sent Albert a note that said, "Waiting for what? What for?" I signed it "Tasti."

I didn't hear back.

Of the two of us, Albert had always been the grifter, but in the end it was I who had learned better than he how to shank people.

I sat in the courtroom with my schoolteacher haircut, and my schoolteacher sports jacket. Annetta was beside me with her face held clear and proud of me, or sometimes with her eyes down and teary. Our son made a shy appearance of about a half hour one morning session. The D.A.'s idea.

On the other side of the room Albert slouched, his hair outlandishly greased back against style, his lips pressed forward in permanent contempt for all of us—for the judge, and the lawyers, but mostly for me. The trial lasted for seven days and he never gave any of us even a small piece of himself.

And so the jury had liked me better. And so had sent him to jail.

August 15, 1973, out by the garage:

"*Albert.*

"*Albert, back when the two of us were talking about Joe D. and Ali, personal morality—responsibility—I never figured we'd have to use it for real, did you? And so soon too.*

"*You listening to me, Albert? Can you hear me from up there? How are things in Dannemora? That's a joke, son. You got anything to say? Would you have anything to say, if you're sitting right here, next to me?*

"*Hey, you know, I was driving up to see you, but I broke down. My Malibu. Oil all over the engine block. Burning and smelling. I had to get it towed.*

"*I got a kick, during the trial, out of when they asked you if you ever carried a human body in your trunk. You told them no, but how about yourself, in the trunk of the Fleet, eating a sandwich on April Fools Day? Cheese sandwich, I think? You remember that? With me driving, you back there eating.*

"*But you're doing all right up there, right? You're getting by at least, surviving? So.*

"*So anyway, Albert, you gotta listen to me, okay? You hearing me now? Listen, kid, you're my brother, all right? Always. You know that. We're closer than that. Closer. Hey, okay? What I do to you, I'm the same time I'm doing it to myself, you understand? Albert, what I did, when I went to the cops, when I worked with the lawyers, I was driving a nail through my own hand. My own palm there, Albert. You understand me? You listening from up there? You're the one who's doing the years up there, Albert, this I know, but that's MY blood too spilled there on the floor. My hands. My blood.*

"You believe me? Albert, I got a wife, and I got a family down here on the Island. I gotta do right by them, I gotta do right by myself, don't I? I mean, I'm down here, without a car, I'm talking to you, trying to talk, just trying to get you to see what happened. How it all came out, see? Please. My wife and my kid, they're down here crying, it seems, all the time now. And I'm out here by the garage trying to make some kind of peace.

"Albert, can you do the time? You'll be able to survive through it, will you? How bad is it? It's just like basic training, I bet, but all the time, right?

"Albert?

"Albert, you know, forgiveness is a powerful thing. It can be a weapon even. Albert, 'la miglior vendetta e' il perdono.' That's Italian. Says it's the best revenge. Forgiveness is.

"Albert, how bad is it up there? Hey?

"Well. Okay then, now, I'm going back in the house."

SIXTEEN

IT WAS MY guess that the thing that most disturbed Albert about living an imprisoned existence would be the neatness of it all. For his whole life, he had paid wallowing homage to the gods of disarray. His warehouse had been a shrine to disorder. True, he could quickly find any wrench, any record album or eight-track, any baby mobile in stock, but that wasn't because of a system or because of organization. It was because he understood chaos, not wall charts.

His whole life on the outside had been that way. He never went to sleep at a preordained hour. Some days he didn't go to sleep at all. His next meal could be a French five-courser, or a doughnut with the green-spotted part held underneath so that he wouldn't have to look at it when he bit. Sometimes his meal would be nothing at all, just good conversation and laughter.

Women he dated had to get used to not knowing when he would pick them up, or when they would get back home. Or where they would be in the meantime. Dress for the beach, wind up at a party. Get caught wearing bowling shoes at a wedding.

From what I knew and saw about prison life, from between the cracks in the walls and the spaces between the bars, life inside was built on regimen. Maybe the dough-nuts had no green mold on them, but they were always the same—powdered sugar—and always available at seven-thirty in the morning, every morning.

Albert must have hated that.

I don't know this for sure, because Albert wouldn't talk to me during his incarceration.

I would sit out in the alley, with my back leaning on the garage by our apartment, and I would speak to him. Figuring out things I should be telling him. Him 300 miles upstate, sitting lonely in a cell.

But, like *Compare* Biaggo during those fake seances

that my Uncle Rocco and Uncle Zippy used to run, Albert never spoke back, he never answered me.

New York decided that Albert would be a state-secured inmate housed at the Clinton Correctional Facility, known to most of the state as Dannemora. It was way the hell upstate.

Annetta and I began trying to get her pregnant again. We both hoped that it would help things between us. We had never been closer than we had been during the time right after James Albert was born.

I worked a second job as a security guard for a couple months, until I got fired. Annetta and I would need a few extra bucks if we were to have another kid. We'd need a bigger place eventually. Annetta started working at the Publishers Clearing House, in Port Washington. Things were pretty busy for us both.

Another school year started up. The teachers all treated me like I had been wronged by Arlynn; like I was a co-victim of the tragedy. The students didn't even know the story.

I took on an extra job assignment as drama advisor and was amazed at how much time it took to put on a student production. We were doing *The Glass Menagerie*.

A couple of months into Albert's incarceration, this very stupid idea came to me and it stuck. The only excuse I can offer is—I had been reading *The Count of Monte Cristo* with my classes, three times a day. And so I decided to do this—I would take control of Albert's empire—his warehouse and his string of girls—and I would build up the business and I would present it all back to him, now worth millions, as we met again at the prison gate after his out-processing, whenever it would be.

The plan, naturally, was a fiasco. Not only couldn't I build up Albert's string of prostitutes, I couldn't even find them.

Without seeing any listings in the Yellow Pages, or television ads with phone numbers, I had no idea how to make contact with Albert's girls.

I remembered Albert telling me that a few of his prime areas were in Seacliff, so I went over there and hung around. I was leaving a bar when a girl about twenty, dressed in a miniskirt and Mets jersey and sneakers, stopped me on the street. She made a pretense out of asking me for directions.

"So, you work around here?" I asked. I was trying to let her know that I was scoping her out, but I had never quite gotten the knack of how that worked. I felt more like Ben Turpin than Clark Gable.

"No. Well, I work all around, not just around here," she told me.

"I bet you do."

"What?"

"I said I bet you do. Work all around. Maybe you could work for me for a little while."

"I don't think so."

"Aren't you one of Albert Niklozak's girls?"

"No," she said, "Ralph Nader."

She was a college student conducting surveys on consumerism and the environment for an advocate organization. I filled out one of her surveys before we said our good-byes.

My track record with prostitutes was not very productive. Years before I had been to an educational convention in Boston and had been walking back to the hotel, thinking about the presentation I had just heard. A painted woman stopped me and asked, "Hey, you wanna go upstairs?"

I said to her, "What for?"

What for.

My efforts to protect Albert's interests in the warehouse fared no better. I wrote Lupo a few letters, got no reply, then tried to get a lawyer of my own to look into it. But I didn't have the finances. I tried to interest the lawyer in a percentage thing somehow.

Fiasco.

One evening, I decided to go down there to the warehouse in person. I had been in the Raspberry Lounge for a couple hours, buying drinks for Benny "The Mutt" Kelleher, who years before had been The Green Hornet that Albert had beaten in the game of Horse. Now Benny the Mutt got drunk each night on his way home from his day of making boxes down at the box plant.

He told me, "Y'know, sometimes a bottle of booze can be a relic of redemption."

I told him, "Yes, it could."

I explained to him how I believed Lupo and the Yacovazzis were cheating Albert out of his rightful possessions. The Mutt agreed with me. Finally after a couple more bracers, we made up our minds to go down there and let them all know that we were acting as Albert's emissaries. They'd have to deal with *us* from now on.

As I got out of the car, across the street from the warehouse, the Mutt, who was driving, said to me, "I'll pick you up."

"What'd you mean?"

"I'll drop you off here, I'll pick you up later. Call me up when you're done. I'll come get you."

"You chicken-shit, c'mon."

The Mutt drove off. I stumbled over to the warehouse and started pounding on the door. Everybody had left hours ago.

Sober, I wrote a letter to Albert explaining what it was I had tried to do for him, and I told him of my frustrations. In the letter, I made myself sound like a real schmoe, but he already knew that. Trying to give him a laugh.

Before I signed the letter, I wrote in, "I know how you hate my guts. I knew you would when I did what I did. But I did not have any other choice. If anybody was in my place, they would have to do the same thing. I just want you to tell me you understand. Even just partially. Even just a little bit. It would mean a lot to me. Albert, even just a couple words would mean a lot to me."

When the comedian Jackie Vernon got depressed early in his career, he would sit down and write a letter to his idol, Charlie Chaplin, who was an expatriate by then. Jackie wrote hundreds of letters, never got an answer back from the Little Tramp. Finally, years later, after Jackie had made a name for himself in comedy, he met Chaplin face to face. As they were being introduced, Chaplin looked up and asked him, "Why'd you stop writing?"

I wrote letter after letter to Albert. I never stopped writing. Albert never wrote back.

In my classroom, I used to tell the kids this joke. William Cullen Bryant wrote "To a Waterfowl." But he died a broken man, because the waterfowl never wrote back.

James Albert and I had a little birthday celebration for Annetta. It was one of those nights when everything she did annoyed me. After I'd put James Albert to bed and come back to the living room, she made some casual reference to Albert.

"Let me ask you something," I said to her, loud, "I know you two were lovers back then, before we met. I know you did. So how can you just abandon him now?"

She said, "Jay, I dated Albert *three* times. Exactly three. Baby, you're losing control of yourself. If I can't help you, and you can't help yourself, then we have to try to find a way."

I told her I didn't think so.

I went up to Dannemora during Christmas break. I signed my name in the visitors' log, told the guard Albert's name, and I waited.

The visitors' room reminded me of a school cafeteria. Twenty plastic one-piece picnic style tables and seats were crowded into the room of tiled floor and bricked walls. The bricks ended three-quarters of the way up the wall. From there, white sheetrock held lousy murals picturing fields and oceans. I presumed that the murals had been done by the prisoners. Donuts were piled on the tables, but the room smelled like cheese.

The guard came back and told me that Albert was unavailable.

"Unavailable? What's that mean? What else is there for him to do around here?"

The guy just looked at me. He looked like a high school kid.

I asked him, "But he's in the building, right?"

He didn't laugh.

"Look, sir, just tell me this, this is Albert Niklozak's choice, not to come out? Not to see me?"

He said, "Yes, sir. It is."

I said, "I come all the way up. Well, I guess he's plenty busy." I was about to leave, when I turned back and asked the guard if he could deliver a note. He made a face, but agreed to.

I wrote, "Please, Albert, I came all the way up. We don't even have to talk about anything much, if you don't want to. I'd just like to see you. See for myself that you're OK."

I was glad to see the guard finally coming back; more glad when he handed me a piece of paper. It was the only time Albert had communicated with me since he'd written, "I'm waiting."

The note the guard handed me was folded over three or four times, smaller than a postage stamp. I unfolded it, read it once.

It read, "Kiss my rocks."

It was a phrase we used to use as kids; you'd only say it to someone you held in no esteem.

The following summer, I drove back up to prison. Albert had been in for almost a year by then. I had been writing him about once a week. I kept hoping that I could tell him that Annetta was pregnant again. I didn't have much else to say.

This time he came out to me in the visitors' lounge. I forced myself to keep looking at him as he did his jail house strut across the room to the table where I was sitting. I didn't stand up.

He looked much smaller to me, almost slight. His hair was still greased back, unchanged. His face was white, with loose skin and acne scars that I didn't remember. His eyes seemed cloudy, holding black puffs of skin beneath them.

As he sat down across the table from me, I said, "What, you got no tattoos, man? I thought that was the thing up here." I tried to smile.

He said to me, "Tasti, I came out here, I'm waiting to hear you say one thing." He held up one finger.

"What, Albert? What is it? I'm sorry? That I'm sorry? You know that. I'll tell that to you a million times."

Albert said, "That ain't it."

I leaned unto the table with my elbows. "What then? What you want me to say?"

He looked away from me. I told him, "Albert, I don't know what to say. Albert, I'm a family man, I got a wife and kid, named after you. I gotta be down there taking care of them, but all I can think about is you up here. Albert, please. Listen. *La miglior vendetta e' il perdono.* That's Italian. Forgiveness is the best revenge. Can you forgive me, Albert? Can you?"

He got up and walked back to his cell.

I visited the penitentiary at Dannemora a few more times after that, once the next spring, once at the beginning of the summer.

Then I stopped going up there for good.

Sometimes I would think about Albert in his neat little cell upstate, maybe him sitting there thinking about me.

I kept writing him letters, but they didn't say the right thing. I didn't know what it was that he wanted me to say. There was one key, one phrase, if I said it, things would be okay. But I couldn't figure out what it was. It was like trying to find a baseball by rolling your body across the thick, high weeds off third base. It was like trying to find a body that did not want to be found. I could not uncover what Albert wanted me to say.

I kept writing anyway. Maybe Albert would finally write a letter back to me. Maybe he'd not even mention the past gone bad; he'd just ask me to come on up to Dannemora again. To shoot the shit. Talk about the old times. About Buster Cook and Scout the dog. Shit like that.

Or maybe he'd write to me telling me that he'd been paroled, that things had gotten sped up, that he was due to get out pretty soon. Maybe he'd tell me the date, and the time, and he'd ask me to meet him at the front gate, and I could take him back down state through the Bronx, over the Throgs Neck Bridge, back down to Long Island, back to Duck Alley.

Then maybe I would write back to him—Kiss my rocks.

❖

July 1, 1965, at the bowling alley:

"Tasti, it's Cagney, for sure, you shitting me?"

"Oh, Cagney, Cagney sure, you're quite correct. Cagney could walk the last mile, take that final walk, like nobody else ever could. Nobody."

"Oh, sure, yeah. Practice. Something like that takes years of practice."

"Hey, he did it all the time."

"Sure. That guy walked the last mile every movie he ever made."

"I mean, I think it was in his contract, with the movies. Last reel, Cagney'd have the prison grays on, walking tough down the cell block, the parson walking there with him praying, warden saying some crap, I don't know, maybe that the pardon didn't come in from the governor, Cagney just as cool could be."

"Every time. Except this once I saw, he'd promised a kid's mother he'd piss and shit the whole way—just acting, so the kid'd see it and reform himself. You see that one?"

"I saw this one he was a songwriter or something, danced and sang the whole movie with Ginger Rogers. He wore tuxedo the whole damn movie. But, come that last scene, there he was, wearing prison gray, getting strapped down, getting fried. Didn't make any sense, with the rest of the movie, I mean the worst thing he ever did was write a bad song or something, or to dance with someone who wasn't Ginger, so I guess they fried him for that. Was in his contract, every movie."

"Yeah, could be."

"Luis Arroyo, walking in from the bull pen, did it the same way. Cool."

"Tasti, that's how we're gonna do it, our time comes, when we get a few more years on us. Am I right?"

"Yeah, but our time will never come. We're too cool."

"You know who else walked the final mile the way it oughta be walked, I was thinking?"

"Who's that?"

"Pete."

"Pete, Pete who? Who's Pete, Pete the barber?"

"No, Pete, you know Pete. Pete the parakeet."

"Albert, could you please, if we're talking here about something?"

"No, no, listen. Pete, as you remember, he hung himself. I'm not saying that's the thing to do. All I'm saying, the poor thing's depressed, been locked up so long . . ."

"Albert. Albert. Your bird got his head wrapped up in his cuttlebone string, which was there tying his cuttlebone to the bars because you were too cheap to buy a cuttlebone holder. This bird did not choose death of his own volition."

"Locked up. Crumby little cage. His own shit all over the floor there. I shoulda cleaned up more. He couldn't take it no more. I'm not saying it's right. I'm saying he didn't piss and moan about it, he just went out and did something about it."

"Yeah, Albert, sure, sure, he flew south. Who else? Who else walked the final mile in style?"

"Wallenda. What's his name, Karl?"

"The tightrope guy?"

"Yeah, King Karl and that whole family. Always falling, busting themselves all up. One fall, about fifteen of them, four-five generations, they're raining, I mean, it's RAINING fucking Wallendas right there in the circus tent. Karl's on his way down, hasn't even hit sawdust yet, he's already thinking how many hospital days before they'll let him climb back up there."

"Yeah, I remember that. Couple years ago it was."

"Doing the Seven. They were doing the Seven, man, three decks high, unbelievable. They all fell in Detroit, I think it was. Fucking Detroit was COVERED with bloody Wallendas."

"Yeah. The act lost some of its impact after that, I bet, when they had to string TWO tightropes instead 'a just one, couple feet apart, so they could take the tires off Karl's wheelchair, have him ride the wire on his rims. Crowd was embarrassed by it, I'm sure."

"You wanna go a frame? They're empty now."

"Nah. Nope. What're you thinking?"

"I'm thinking, twenty, thirty, fifty, a hundred years from now— it's my time to go—I'll go out like Cagney, or a tightrope walker. Hell, I'll go out like Pete the parakeet."

"So, Albert, why is it tonight, if I may ask, tonight you're so concerned with the final walk all of a sudden? What got you thinking? I think I know, but I'm asking."

"Yeah, you know. You're right. I'm not afraid to say it. We're getting feeling pretty good, but we ain't sloppy yet. I'm off to Fort Hamilton, for processing, Friday, what's that, day after tomorrow, no, it's after midnight already, so it's tomorrow I'm gone. You're off to where? Lackland, off to Texas, right after me, after that. After that, we're proba- bly both of us'll be probably in Nam, before the end of the year, where there's people, I got to point out, intending on killing us if they can catch us. Little crazy fuckers, protect- ing their own country, rubber slippers and house coats, yel- low skin in black silk, intent on killing us, because that's where they live. And you know what, friend, they'll succeed at it too, for some of us, they'll succeed. Maybe not you and me, God hopes, but they'll be successful in their attempts to kill some big, white, big-eyes, big-ass invaders. Maybe they'll even kill you and me. We don't know who, at this point, we only know some. Some of us will die, old buddy, so, I guess, who knows, is what I'm saying, right? Who fucking knows?"

"Yeah. Who."

"So, all I'm saying is, if it's me gets killed, I want to go out like Pete the parakeet. I want to take my final walk just like that brave little birdie did."

SEVENTEEN

ALBERT WAS BEATEN to death in prison by three black investment advisors using pipes.

I heard about it first from Bobby Gallaga—he called me up—but I would not accept it for awhile. Albert was thirty-one years old, just like me.

I phoned Ron Cloud Carlini. He listened with patience, then he told me, yeah, he'd heard about Albert's beating death too. And so it was true.

I asked Ron Cloud how I could find out what had happened, exactly. I didn't want to talk to anyone in Albert's family. They wouldn't answer me anyway. Ron Cloud said he'd ask around and get back to me. He was being pretty good about it. I hung up, dazed beyond control.

I went into the kitchen and rummaged through the junk drawer, looking for my Pennsy Pinkie. I had forgotten that I had thrown it over the roof tops right before I had turned Albert in to the cops.

I drove down to Lampstons and bought another ball, the closest I could get to the old one. But when I was back out there by the garage, I only threw it twice before I grabbed it and tried to rip it into halves. I couldn't do it, my hands kept slipping in sweat; I couldn't see too well.

So instead, I crumpled down into the gravel and the pavement of the alley. Annetta told me later that some neighbors saw me out there and called her up. I don't remember her coming out to get me or bringing me back into the apartment. I don't know how long I was out there.

All that night I sat in a chair in the living room scratching my leg until it bled. Annetta finally went to bed.

A couple days later, Ron Cloud called me back with a name and the telephone number of an ex-con who he said could tell me about Albert. A guy named Johnson; he had just gotten paroled and was trying to stay on the good side of the D.A.'s office, so he'd agreed to talk to me. Ron Cloud said that this Johnson could probably tell me the facts of why, how, Albert was dead.

For three straight days I didn't go out of the apartment. I just scratched my leg and called the guy's number until I finally made contact. He was living in a sort of halfway house off Utopia Parkway in Queens. I went in there to meet him. It was right by where I had gone to college.

The guy answered the door, told me his house mates were out, and he sat me down at a paint-chipped metal table in the kitchen. He asked me if I wanted a glass of water.

He was a very slender little guy, of maybe forty hard years, as black as anyone could come, with huge eyes and lips and a voice so soft and nice it was like singing when he spoke. He grinned, showed broken teeth and a blackened gum line, and he told me that his name was Boy-Girl Johnson. His sweet-voiced words started coming razor-quick, and I had some trouble understanding all of them.

"I be Albert Nickels' bunkie," he told me. "We two, same cell up there for while, that shitty place, you know what I sayin?"

He told me that the three investment advisors who had beaten Albert to death with pipes were all bad-ass inmates. He called them niggers. They had started out as crooked financial dealers on the outside. Once inside, the three of them had adapted. All three had been inmates in the same wing as Albert and Boy-Girl. From what Boy-Girl told me, they usually contracted out any blood-letting that they deemed necessary, but this time, Boy-Girl had heard, they decided to bloody their own hands.

"They run the wifes for the whole entire wing, you understand? Maybe for the whole rest of the place too, that I do not know. But where *we* was, man, Albert Nickels and me, they three run it all. Okay? Guy want a wife, you pay these, they supply the ass, you understand? What it is I sayin to you?"

208

I told him I did.

"About what I be sayin to you? To you?"

"Yeah. If a guy wanted sex from another inmate, these guys were in control of it, right?"

"That right. You got it."

I said, "Okay then."

Boy-Girl told me, "I their first wife, first one they ever had. When they was first gettin started up in business up there. See, they real smart businessmen, they been on Wall Street and all. They got put in for doin things with numbers, things you, me, we would not even understand if they told us. You understand? The corpor-ate numbers, for the brothers, did not add up. Plus, racism. So they get inside, they gotta still be businessmen, right? Different business, that's all. But me, I be their first, from the first. I be openin up my cheeks on consignment, they takin care of my stock. Stock and trade. Long time."

He stopped talking for a while. He looked at me; I just took a breath and nodded.

"The people callin me Boy-Girl though, not for that, for another reason. If you wonderin. That even before I go in, my name. It's cause of my sweet pipes, you understand? On account of how it is I talk. But now, see, I ain't gonna do no testifyin. I ain't gonna name no names. I just get out, couple days, since right around when Albert Nickels die, so I be walkin straight, I just here talkin to you, man to man, right?"

"That's fine. That's all I want."

"Ron Cloud he say you just wanna talk, find out things for you-self. You a cop? Ron Cloud, the D.A., he say no. I ask you, you a cop, sir?"

"What?"

"You look too scrawny be a cop."

"I'm a schoolteacher."

"On, yeah, that ain't much."

"No, well."

"Oh so, better than nothin. Fuckin schoolteacher. Oh, well, that okay. Why you askin? You not blood."

"About Albert?"

"Bout Albert Nickels, and how he die, why you been askin?"

"He was my friend."

"Oh, yeah?"

Boy-Girl Johnson asked me for a cigarette, I shook my head. He slapped his sides, then took a butt out of his shirt pocket and lit it. He said to me, "Albert Nickels you friend. He my friend too."

Boy-Girl started telling me about how he and Albert had shared a cell, had hated each other for awhile, then became buddies. He said there was a lot of time to talk in prison. Boy-Girl was there for dealing heroin. I asked him if he knew why Albert was in.

"One time we talkin bout why we two been locked. He tell me bout the body they find all buried up, I say to Nickels, I tell him, 'Man, you don't kill so good, do ya,' Nickels, he say to me, 'I kill fine, man, if I ever have to, it's my *buryin'* what needs work.'"

Boy-Girl stopped to laugh awhile. "I say to him, 'What you talkin about?' He say, 'Boy-Girl, I wanna kill somebody, then I kill em, if I gotta, that's all. But I never kill this girl, never, ever. To be up here, at all.'"

I leaned forward and asked, "So he talked about the killing, huh? The burying of the body?"

"Wha?"

"He spoke to you about killing and burying the girl?"

Boy-Girl said, "No. Just that. Just what I say."

Boy-Girl mostly wanted to talk about Albert's death.

"See, like I say, them boys don't usually do it themself. They get it done through channels. But with Nickels, they feel very personal about. He give em a hard time. You see, I got me religion, what it was, you understand? I got me religious, right at the right time, didn't wanna be no one's boy-girl no more, even though that my name, cause I got religion, right time, but I got the wrong *kind*, see?"

"What?"

"If you ever in prison, school-teach, let me tell you some advice— if you gotta get religion, get Muslin. Every time. If you can't, and you still gotta get religion, well then, least get you-self Baptist. Ain't as good as Muslin, but least you won't get you-self tooken to the shower with pipes and sharp metal, you hear me? But see, my trouble, I don't go listenin to my own damn advice. I got religion, you know what kind I got? I got *Catholic*. Yeah, some bald, red-face priest dude talk me into it in the day room, then later on back at his office. See, that my mistake. You in prison, you gotta get a sickness, say, well, get a flu, get a cold, get a fever blister there on you lip. Don't get nothin'll kill you, cancer or leukemia or nothin. Don't matter where you at, don't go gettin nothin like that. Well, same thing with religion. You in prison, you gotta get religion, get Muslin, get Baptist, don't go gettin no fuckin Catholic. I got *Roman* Catholic too, like there be some other kind. There be any other kind? There is, I never even hear of it. But Catholic ya see, when you doin time, Catholic it ain't even on the board. Cause all this means is, you God ain't gonna come and raise a powerful hand to slew the tide of these bastards come to screw you up with metal objects. I look around, I say—no more mister boy-girl action for this Mr. Boy-Girl, I say that, here they come after me, they carryin metal, and my God the big bad-ass Catholic, that boy ain't nowheres around. I say I ain't gonna do no more wife-action no more, they say yeah, you are. I be gettin out in a couple days, they don't care, they still gonna make their point. I'm gettin tooken down to the shower, to be sodomed, gommorahed, all of it, my Catholic God ain't there steppin in. The only one steppin in for me, it's Albert. It's Mr. Cell-man, my man, my friend, Mr. Albert the Nickel. He a good, brave, tough, loyal cocksucker, but you know what? Jesus Christ on the cross woulda been able to take a beatin and still be tickin, He done it once. But my man Nickels, he can't do that. His skull too thin, his bones too weak. He bleed too much. Like a ordinary man, cause that what he was. School-teach, he lyin on the tiles on the shower there, the water turnin red with Nickel blood, everybody know—this ain't no God lyin there. This ain't no Jesus Christ. This ain't no Allah. This be a man. Lyin, dyin, bleedin. Dyin for his fellow man, which in this case, it happen to be me, you understand what it is I sayin?"

Back when Albert and I were about eleven, the kids three or four years older than us controlled the neighborhood. They had arranged a gang fight with the Back Lots and they recruited us to help out with a few of the more mundane jobs. We accepted, coveting their mantle.

The big kids had built a fort—really just four walls made out of tongue and groove flooring nailed to the sides of four conveniently located trees. One wall had a window cut out of it—a two-foot square framed opening. My job was to stand inside the window and when they'd get a Back Lots kid dragged to the window, I was supposed to reach out and grab him around the neck in a choke hold as the kids outside worked his face and body. I had pretty strong arms for a skinny eleven-year old.

I don't remember what job Albert was assigned, but I remember standing, screaming, crying hot tears, as I watched two big kids with head locks on each other twisting around on the dirt floor of the fort. I felt helpless and useless, just wanted to get out of there.

Mr. McQuillen stopped the big rumble by coming to the edge of the woods where we were and yelling at us. All the kids paused in mid-action, listened to him, then started home.

Praying to God that my eyes weren't red, I listened to Albert describing what a great time he had been having.

Whether my friend was wearing a propeller beanie into a tough section of Queens, or just fighting with the Back Lots as an eleven-year-old in the woods of Duck Alley, Albert had always enjoyed the contact. The giving and taking, dishing it or covering up—he felt most alive during a good knuckling.

Driving back out from Boy-Girl's place in Queens, I tried to convince myself that Albert had died fighting, died doing what he liked doing. Maybe that's something all of us aspire to. He was a man who had enjoyed pimping, who had died at the hands of pimps when one of their string didn't want to do it anymore. Boy-Girl had found religion, and chose to walk away from the degradation. And his friend Albert Niklozak, ex-pimp, had stood by him. And I hoped that Albert had felt a sense of right about all of this, as he died.

As I pulled my car into the driveway, I knew all of these ideas were absurd. Albert had simply been beaten to death in prison by three black investment advisors using pipes.

Sitting in bed, sweating through my pajama top, eyes opened, I studied forms that were moving across the dark. When I got to sleep hours later, I was jolted back upright by the memory: Albert's last living communication with me, filled with jail house seething, had been, "Tasti, I came out here, I'm waiting to hear you say one thing." He had held up one finger.

And when I told him I was sorry, he said, "That ain't it."

❖

213

June 30, 1974, in the visitors' room:

"Albert, la miglior vendetta e' il perdono."

EIGHTEEN

SILENCE CAN BE the most noble of human conditions.

Back in Duck Alley, even after the Niklozaks got television, Albert would come over to my house, claim his spot on our couch, and we'd watch wrestling. Sometimes my uncles would watch with us, sometimes not. My grandmother would be in the kitchen, or upstairs, my father would be working or sitting by himself out on the porch.

Our favorite wrestler was Tony "The Silent Man" Pontonelli. Albert usually went for the bad guys, but we both loved Tony, the goodest of the good. Tony was the *galantuomo* of his profession, the consummate gentleman, a serene stroller in a world of loud-mouthed strutters, and he probably didn't win more than twenty matches in twenty years.

It was the Golden Age of Wrestling and Tony mostly worked the Northeast circuit, from "Bedlam in Boston" to Armory Hall. His charge in this grunting and groaning universe was to be sacrificial meat for the up and coming bad guys, the blow-hards. They who would be gaining—at Tony's expense—exposure, experience, and enough crowd enmity to fill up the Gardenside Arena for the big, non-televised, championship and challenge matches at $4.50 a head and up.

So each televised Tuesday, with me and Albert cheering but knowing what was to come, Silent Tony would be knocked unconscious by table legs wielded like baseball bats by the Kilodny Twins; or have his eyeballs scraped by the piece of glass that the Blood Sheik always kept hidden in his trunks but that the ref never saw; or get a Super-Wedge from Bad Boy Bobby Naughton; or have his head smashed into the turnbuckle, face first, by Nazi Jack Schmidt. Yet Tony silently endured.

Who knows, maybe that was where Albert first learned how it was to be done.

Only once in a great while would Tony appear to lose his temper. He would bring someone like Genghis Kohn to his cowardly knees, begging for mercy. And Tony would actually consider granting him that mercy. Tony would bring back his fist but he would hold it there, as Genghis would raise up his palms in supplication.

Then, instead of letting that fist fly into that subhuman piece of tartar sauce, Tony would turn to us and ask, "Should I do it, audience? Should I do it?" He wasn't just playing to the crowd, he was really asking.

"Yeah, nail him, nail the bastard," the standing, sweating hysterical crowd would yell back. "Let 'er fly." Thousands of us were watching at home and Tony couldn't hear us, but we would be telling him too, in accents Italian and Hungarian, Irish and Slavic, and sometimes second generation with no accent at all except maybe city-kid or suburb. Uncle Rocko would roll forward in his chair, yelling at the cathode tube, desperately trying to get the message through.

"Should I do it?" Tony would ask us again, his fist still back and poised, but by then, of course, it would be too late. Genghis would rip a terrible punch into Silent Tony's crotch, and then follow that with a head butt or lip twist, and then an obvious choke hold that would turn Tony's ephemeral moment of authority into something cold and numb, wet and gone, silent.

It only upset us for a moment. This was, after all, Tony. What else would we expect? He would never break a rule, or bend one, no matter what the rest of the world was capable of. And we wanted to be like that.

All Tony had going for him were his code of silence—*omerta*—and his impenetrable stomach muscles. Time, robbing his body of elasticity and strength, couldn't soften that magnificent stomach. During the ringside interviews, when Bruno or Bobo would be posturing and bragging, posing and gesturing, trying to grab the microphone, Tony would quietly state that he had never been hurt in the mid-section. Harry Houdini might have been killed that way, but Tony's stomach was his Iron Curtain. That's what he called it—getting as close to a brag as he would ever come—his Iron Curtain.

So it was no surprise that when the Mad Lithuanian challenged Tony to take one of his deadly Atom Bomb Drops to the stomach, Tony said, "Sure, why not."

As Tony entered the ring that night, smiling and waving to the fans, the fathers in the crowd leaned over and told their sons about Tony and his stomach, and the sons nodded. Tony lay down on the canvas, beside the ropes, flexing those marvelous box muscle—taut, perfectly defined, completely motionless.

Then the Lithuanian climbed between the ropes, growling at the crowd and showing his armpits. He made a few derogatory gestures at Tony, went over and re-positioned Tony and the box muscles slightly, and climbed up to the middle rung.

Holding on with both hands and feet, the Lithuanian began bouncing up and down on the rope, going faster and higher with each bounce; there was a psychotic grin playing somewhere in his scraggly beard.

Tony lay motionless below him—mid-section flexed— his eyes gently closed.

Then, just as it appeared that the rope was nearly at its breaking point, the Lithuanian leaped off, up into the air, using the tension of the rope to sling-shot his body at least ten feet above the canvas.

At the apex of the leap, he curled himself into a hard, massive bundle, completely spherical except for the point of one brutal knee extending out below. That knee was aimed at the motionless body of the Silent Man. This was the Atom Bomb Drop.

The Lithuanian missile began its descent, gaining speed at the rate of sixteen feet per second per second, all of the momentum of the 285-pound-body focused into that one, terrible, hard-boned knee.

Tony did not flinch. The crowd noise must have told him exactly what was happening, but he kept his concentration on his stomach muscles. Ring-siders, looking for a hint of uncertainty or fear, found none. I like to think that Tony was viewing this moment from outside of himself, from outside of his concentration. He was silently viewing all of it as his final victory, the victory of his own *vis vitae*, the victory of silent nobility over infamy.

His Iron Curtain, with a show of invincibility, would atone for the years of pain and suffering and humiliation.

And, as the Lithuanian's knee cut the distance between itself and Tony in half, again and again, closer and closer, the crowd released as one a gasp that was full of awe and fear and expectation and, in one last terrifying instant, the knee landed, with its full crushing impact.

Directly on Tony's throat.

Albert and I were witness to that ignominious event on Channel 5, the Dumont Network. It so impressed us that we both immediately decided to become sports commentators. We would take turns doing our commentary on the incident, adding different phrases and flavors each time through.

Finally we took the old reel-to-reel tape recorder that one of my uncles had bought at a rummage sale, and we spent hours reciting our Silent Tony commentary and then doing other sporting events, as we watched them on television with the sound turned down.

I hadn't gone to Albert's funeral. No one would have wanted me there.

Later, Bobby Gallaga told me that a bunch of the old crowd was setting off Roman Candles that night, to remember Albert.

I didn't go to that either, but I stood a few blocks over and watched the fireworks lighting up the sky above Duck Alley. I could hear the whoosh as they took off.

In *The Glass Menagerie*, a guy working in a shoe ware-house abandons his sister to become a writer. But her image never leaves his memory. He says, "Oh, Laura, Laura, I tried to leave you behind me, but I am more faithful than I intended to be."

Finally then, I allowed myself to go on living by reminding myself constantly, hourly, that all of the horrors that I had been witness to had been predicated by Albert's nature for violence. Things had curled in upon themselves, twisted tightly into their own core, and at that rotted core was the lonesome death of Arlynn Svenson.

Sure, I had been the rat in all of this, and I was paying for that by not getting more than two straight hours of sleep since it had all begun. But still, sometimes the dreams which stung me awake were strange yet also soft, almost gentle, quiet, based on things that we had seen back in Duck Alley, based on better times. Most of the time they were unspeakable in their horror, but how much worse they would have been if I had allowed Arlynn Svenson's death to go unheeded. Right?

Remember this, Jay Tasti: Albert Niklozak lay dead on the cold porcelain floor of the Clinton Correctional Facility communal shower stall, with all waters running and a choir singing outside to cover the sounds, because his overheated blood had caused Arlynn Svenson to lie dead in the fallen leaves and the mud of Newburgh, New York.

Still though, some of the soft, quick words that Boy-Girl Johnson had said confused me; I kept trying to solve these one or two things.

When he had sat with Albert in their cell and told Albert that he must be a lousy killer, Albert had denied it and answered him, "No, it's my burying that needs work."

Albert had told Boy-Girl that D.A.'s don't care who it is they convict, as long as they get a conviction. That it was a numbers deal. As long as their numbers were good, they're fine. Albert said to Boy-Girl, "I should not be here."

What did that mean? Yes, institutionalization, especially in a place like Dannemora, was supposed to change a man, change the way he walked and held himself, change the way he thought and spoke and tattooed his body, but this wasn't Albert talking. Vietnam had changed some things about Albert too, but nothing anywhere could ever change what was there at his quiet core.

He had told me, "I'm waiting to hear you say one thing." I didn't know what that one thing was; I had stayed silent.

Albert was a man who took what he had coming, always had. Deny and then shut up. If you lost, you lost. So why was he whining to his effeminate cell-bunkie about not having done the crime? What did that mean?

Maybe nothing. Maybe something.

Boy-Girl had said to Albert, "You here, ain't you? You ain't here? You tellin me, you shouldn't be here, you didn't do the crime, you like everybody else in here too?"

"My trial," Albert said to him, "my case, was born out of misdirection. It was born of deceit and treachery."

Those were the exact three words that Albert used to describe the case against him. I had Boy-Girl repeat the words to me. Misdirection. Deceit and treachery. Like the knee of the Mad Lithuanian getting driven into the throat of Silent Tony Pontonelli.

Boy-Girl asked me, "What he mean by that?"

I told him, "I wish I knew."

The apartment was empty and I decided to try to find the old reel-to-reel tapes that Albert and I had made of sporting events back when we were kids hoping to be Mel Allen. I had heard Albert's voice so much in my life, and then so little, then not at all. I wanted to hear it again, even on tape. And it would give me the kind of pain that I needed.

I kept all of my old tapes in a torn, brown shoe box at the foot of the bedroom closet. I didn't see any reel-to-reels in there at all, only cassettes. I picked up the cassette of Herman's Hermits that Arlynn's father had given me.

I started to drop it back into the shoe box, but the case opened and the cassette fell out. It didn't have a Herman's Hermits label. Instead, it held a faded gold stick-on kind that read, "Audiopak Professional Cassette 90." A type you'd buy blank and record yourself. Arlynn had put the tape into a manilla envelope for me, with the message, "Mr. Tasti, Please think only good thoughts of me as you listen to this. Cooch."

I had come home directly from the classroom the afternoon I found her cassette in the shoe box; hadn't loosened up my tie yet. I felt the flesh heating up inside my collar.

I put the tape into my cassette player in the living room. For a long time after I punched the "Play" button, there was only hiss. I twisted up the volume. Then Arlynn Svenson's voice popped out at me, thunder-clap loud, talking about a hush in the world. I twisted the volume knob back down, re-wound the tape, and I listened as Arlynn spoke to me. She told me what had happened to her. She also spoke to me of violence, silence, and morality.

"There's a kind of hush, all over the world. All over the world tonight.

"Dad just got done with me. It made me feel sick, like I always do. But this time I told him—No more. That one last time, okay, but that was it. I'm growing up. I told him it was time I started acting like an adult lady, like you told me to, remember, Jay?

"He got real mad, because he knew I really meant it. The last time.

"He went out to the garage and got one of those things

you use to take off the tires with. I tried to crawl away for awhile, but I couldn't see where I was going. I hate that big drunk. He's gone now. I have a terrible headache. I'm a mess. I hope he goes out and gets himself killed, but he won't. He always comes back.

"I really don't know if I got a baby inside me or not. I hope I don't, because if I do, it would probably be like Rosemary's Baby. Why couldn't *you* be the father, Jay?

"For a long time now I collected enough pills to fly me away. I just took them all. It felt wonderful. I hope I don't throw up.

"Jay, thank you for being my friend. I'm sorry I embarrassed you when we were at Joneses Beach together. I was just trying to be your friend. Jiggle, jiggle. I hope you miss me. Please don't feel guilty. I don't love you, I'm sorry. I love Peter, who's singing to me right now. Can you hear? The only reason I'm making this tape for you is because Peter probably gets thousands of tapes from girls all over the world every day. Even to this very day, he's still very popular. He'd probably just get it and then put it away and never even listen to it.

"That's why I'm sending it to you instead, Jay. Making it for you, and sending it to you.

"There's a kind of hush, all over the world."

❖

June 30, 1974, in the visitors' room:

"I believe in God, the Father Almighty, Creator of Heaven and Earth. . . .'."
"'Do you? Do you really?'"
"'No, do you?'"

NINETEEN

I CROUCHED DOWN like a catcher, with the soles of my feet dug into the mud of the alley, my back propped against the garage wall where I no longer threw a rubber ball. The jagged brown splotch, bigger than a strike zone, had been drawn there on the shingles by thousands of my dirty pitches. Now it surrounded my head like a halo, an aureole of saintly discolor. A canonization which I did not deserve.

Finally I had been made to understand—the palm of my hand had been forced down upon the red-hot grill of the truth. Even though Albert's last correspondence with me had been a slightly obscene little jail-house tough note about kissing his rocks, his *words* to me had been spoken with care and sympathy. And I understood these words now. I understood what Albert meant.

I knew what it was that he was asking me to do when they were leading him in chains to his death, and he stopped there in front of me just long enough to ask, "Jay, take the stand."

And I knew what he was waiting to hear me say, when he sat across from me in the visitors' room upstate and held up one finger and said, "I'm waiting to hear you say one thing."

I pushed up from the ground there in the alley, digging pebbles into the heel of my hand. I would spend the day searching for graves.

Bobby Gallaga and the obituaries had said that Albert was buried in the Most Blessed Rue. Bobby called me a jerk for not going to the service. He was about the only one left from Duck Alley who would still talk to me. That was because Bobby would gossip with anyone—the worse the better, the way he saw things. To him the purpose of any conversation was to smear and listen to smearing, in order to gather material to smear again. So to him, I was the perfect guy to talk with over a beer.

He had told me that Albert was put down somewhere in the old section of the Rue, the corner of the place where Jericho Turnpike crosses Brotherhood.

I parked there and walked around the green fields of stubble, up and down the rows of gray chunks of granite and marble. The grass had grown up and died around the lower markers, and I remembered working as a temporary at Nassau Knolls, where we summer kids were assigned to trim around headstones when we weren't squaring up grave holes. Back then the only thing we had to use were metal-bladed trimmers, plugged into a loud gas-powered generator. If you got too close to a grave stone, the metal of the blade would catch the corner and the whirling cutter would snap back at your legs. This had happened to me and the blade had dug through my desert boot and cut a chunk out of the top of my left foot. I still have the scar.

I walked the rows now, the aisles, looking for Niklozaks. Bobby Gallaga had told me that they had a little family section, but I couldn't find it. I knew that the brick and stone administration building would have a graph with names and diagrams, but I couldn't get myself to go in there and ask for directions to Albert's grave.

I walked around for maybe an hour as trains passed by on the Long Island tracks that touched the property. Finally I went back to my car.

Arlynn's father had told his story pretty straight; he'd just left out the parts about him regularly sexually penetrating his daughter. That day he had chased and beaten her with a lug wrench, then made sure she was alive, then left her bloodied in the living room and gone out to drink off the rest of the week. Deal with it later. Maybe didn't bother to lock the place up. When he got back, his daughter, her money, a couple suitcases, and her clothes were gone. Fine with him.

225

Later, the cops told him that she hadn't run away, that a guy named Albert Niklozak had beaten his daughter to death and dumped her upstate. Fine with him.

Here's what must have happened.

Albert got to the Svenson house, prepared to clean up my garbage for me. He tried the front door and went in.

He had seen death before. He'd been in Nam and the both of us, as kids, had seen Police Officer John Coote's body. We had been watching Pinky Lee on television over at my house when we had heard three gunshots. Explosions. We both thought it was fireworks, so naturally Albert got excited, dug his fingers into the Venetian blinds and looked out, didn't see anything.

A half hour later we were watching Bilko when the Venetian blinds began flashing red. Albert looked out again and this time he saw a circle of cop cars, lights on. We rushed out and saw the blue-uniformed body of a cop lying on the pavement, spilling more blood than we thought the human body could hold. Blood like quarts of oil from a V-8, spilled out on the street.

So Albert knew dead bodies, and blood.

He had probably gone over to Arlynn's body, maybe checked for what killed her—easy to figure. This girl had been beaten to death. That's how people died in Albert's world. The empty pill bottles on the rug, or in the waste paper basket, would have been overlooked or else meant nothing to him.

Then maybe he'd gone and sat by the telephone there for awhile. Cursing his friend Tasti's name. Thinking about his own way of living life. Deciding what to do. Maybe, a couple times Albert had the phone in his hand, ready to dial.

Arlynn had been laid to rest out on the Island, I forgot the name of the yard, but it was way out there, close to

Smithtown. I took the Expressway out and I did the same thing I had done at the Rue. Spent a foggy hour getting my shoes wet looking for the right name carved in stone. I couldn't find Arlynn's grave either, and this place was a lot smaller than the Rue. Maybe Albert's grave was too new, didn't carry a marker yet, but Arlynn's should have.

I felt as if I had walked every row in the place, read every name and date at least twice. A few of them made me hesitate; the two dates on the stone were so close to each other. Arlynn's dates would have been seventeen years apart, but I didn't find the spot where they had laid her down.

Here's what must have happened.

Albert never dialed the telephone. Instead, he chose silence. He ran a handkerchief over the receiver, tried to touch as few things as possible in the house. In her bedroom, he pulled the thick white embroidered bedspread off the bed, and he brought it back into the living room, where he used it to wrap up Arlynn's now-stiff young body. The blood was coagulating pretty good by now, so it was more goo than flowing.

Albert cracked her limbs into a lying posture, picked her up, and took her out to the trunk of his car. Probably checked the street out first. Then he had to re-snap her body into a folded-up position, so that he could get her all into the trunk and still be able to close it.

Did he think then about our April Fool's gag, when *he* had been the one in the trunk, eating a cheese sandwich, looking back at the car behind? Did the trunk accidentally spring open on his way upstate, like we had it do many years before? Did he have to pull over, go back around, slam it down hard and then drive on?

On my drive back in from Smithtown, I thought about my lesson plans for the next Monday. We were doing Poe, and I always read "The Tell-Tale Heart" out loud to each class. "If still you think me mad, you will think so no longer when I describe the wise precautions I took for the concealment of the body."

Nassau Knolls, where I had dug graves as a kid, didn't have a good place to park my car, so I left it hanging half off the roadway, half on the grass of the graveyard.

This was where my father and grandmother were buried. Uncle Zippy had disappeared, so my Uncle Rocco was living by himself in the old house, rarely going out, seeing people less and less.

I stood over Pa's and Grandma's graves for awhile, with nothing to say. I remembered the digging when I had worked there, and the feel of it on my hands. I forgot to look for the empty holes left by the disinterred Indian, or by Naj Bimbaghulya's husband. What did graveyards do with the empty holes left over after removing bodies? What was the procedure for a hole like that? Does the company resell it? Just fill it in and let it be?

I had to rock the car back and forth a few times to dig its wheels out of the roadside mud of Nassau Knolls.

Here's what must have happened.

Being careful but not careful enough, Albert drove Arlynn's body upstate to his Sunburst of Mountainville dumping grounds and he buried her as best he could.

He dug the hole by himself this time—I wasn't there to help him—and he dug until he got tired. When you're nervous and mad and alone, you get tired out quicker. Maybe he looked up to check the sky, up through the pine tree branches; maybe it was starting to get light out and he only had a trenching shovel that he kept in the trunk. He covered the spot with dead leaves and small branches. He stepped back. It looked pretty good. He went back to the car to clean up the trunk.

He did not know that it would be a wet spring.

As I drove out of Nassau Knolls, I thought about going upstate. I could make it by sundown. I could go trespassing, right behind Sunburst of Mountainville, not for visiting Arlynn's dumping ground but rather looking for the spot where we had buried the Shadow, years before.

I could bring to my mind so much of what had gone on back then—the sights and sounds and feelings of it. I could relive it more readily than things that had happened just a week ago.

I could picture the hillside where we had buried the dog. I could picture it, but I probably couldn't find it.

I drove back home.

Here's what must have happened.

Like the nuns had taught us about Jesus, Albert had died for our sins. And died for our misunderstandings. Albert had accepted his death, gone to it violently, thinking that his friend was a killer.

Once my wife had looked at a grasshopper in our bathroom and seen a cockroach, because that's what she expected in a low-rent apartment. She should have known better. Albert and I had looked at each other and each of us had seen a killer in the other. We both should have known better.

The only difference between my friend and me had been this—when I saw a killer, I turned him in, ratted him out, to the cops and to the D.A. I had allowed my friend to be led through the catacombs of the legal system, to be chained and boarded up like beef, and then to be broken down into death by the three black investment advisors in the shower. Using lead pipes.

Sitting in his jail cell, waiting for his friend to come forth to free him, Albert had been more loyal to our friendship than I ever imagined.

When Albert looked at me and saw a killer, he chose silence. He cleaned up my mess; then he had denied, denied, been a stand-up guy. And when he had asked me to make it right for us— "Jay, take the stand"—he had asked it not for himself, but for me. He saw a killer who was letting his friend carry the cross for him. He had worried more about what that act was doing to his friend than what it was doing to him.

He had said, "Tasti, I came out here, I'm waiting to hear you say one thing." He asked of me, "Jay, take the stand."

Instead, I had gone home and made love to my wife, hoping that for a brief few moments my memory and conscience would leak out of the end of my sweet-sliding shaft.

❖

June 28, 1954, in Duck Alley:

> *"So long."*
> *"G'bye."*
> *"Maybe I'll see you after supper."*
> *"Yeah, maybe."*

TWENTY

As FAR As anyone could remember, my Uncle Zippy didn't know anybody west of the Hudson River. Yet, they found him in Chicago, dead in a rented room, with a prostate full of cancer and two lungs full of pneumonia. His brother Rocco said he'd never forgive him for that.

The last couple years of my own life were pitched at an angle from where I was standing so that I could just stumble forward, using gravity as my driving force. The problem with a life-plan like that is— what you gain in momentum you lose in altitude. Gravity ends at the center of the earth. Still though, at least I was moving.

As a kid, I had dreamed of inventing a Slinky that could run *up* the stairs.

Our drama club at school did *The Glass Menagerie* twice in two years, and Amanda, the mother in the play, told the audience, "Things have a way of turning out so badly."

I went on teaching, or at least doing enough to get a paycheck every other week. Then a fight broke out in the hallway between sixth and seventh periods. It was May and there were always more fights in the spring. This one was a lot more violent than the usual "I'll posture until the teacher gets here and talk tough about it later." This one was for real and I got into the middle of it, the only one around with any interest in doing that.

I realized later that I had enjoyed the physical what-the-hell of it all, just like Albert had always loved a tough knuckler, and at some point during the action I apparently brought a knee up into one of the kid's faces, smashing cartilage flat.

I didn't remember doing it, and I claimed it was an accidental by-product of my overactive peacemaking, but too many witnesses described it differently. I just shrugged it off, had no feelings about it.

My contract wasn't renewed for the next school year. I could have fought it, but I didn't. I remembered Paul Molicki, the drunk who walked the halls with a legal pad and glazed eyes, for years—the zombie of Division High. I told myself I would leave this lousy job before I'd ever let myself become like him. But I realized that I already had.

A janitor gave me a cardboard carton, emptied of text-books, so that I could pack up the stuff from my classroom and desk and from the teachers' room. When I got together all the stuff that I wanted to keep, I didn't need the box. It all fit into my briefcase and my pockets.

Annetta left me, took James Albert with her. Her mother had remarried and moved down to southern Maryland, so Annetta went down there to live and to raise our son.

I was gracious about letting them go. I had made many mistakes with my family, would make more, but every one of them seemed to spring from one fountainhead—my commitment to keeping my mouth shut. When Arlynn Svenson's crazy world had slammed head-first into mine, and her insanity had become a real threat to the life I was living, I should have told Annetta about it. That night, that afternoon, I could have—with just a little bit of discomfort and embarrassment. I could have sat Annetta down and explained the truth, exactly as it had happened.

By the next day it was more difficult to do. The day after that it was impossible.

We don't call each other up much any more, and we never write. She's dating a roofer. I see James Albert three times a year, but it's become like checking the inspection sticker and registration on my car. He's started calling himself Jim.

As it turns out, I can love him more from afar, I think, and maybe better. He knows I can't fly.

Instead of counting teeth with my tongue, I started counting the lives that I'd wrecked or screwed up. Annetta's. James Albert's.

Arlynn Svenson had reached out to me the only way she knew how—tits first—and I had simply put her back onto her incestuous ride to suicide.

Then, when she recorded a death message for me, instead of listening to it, I had tossed it into a shoe box at the bottom of my closet. Another screwed-up life.

Albert's.

My own.

I felt that I should tell someone the truth about Albert— that he wasn't a killer, just a friend—but I could never figure out who to tell. The cops wouldn't care. Ron Cloud. What was left of our Duck Alley crew. What was left of Albert's family. I decided that he would've shrugged and told me, "Fuck it. Forget about it." Forget about it.

I sometimes still visit grave sites. I never did find Albert's grave, or Arlynn's. I drove that circuit a couple more times, but I hardly made it past the statue of Rachel Weeping. I hadn't found those graves when I had first tried. Maybe the next time I would, but I figured it didn't matter. I stopped doing that.

Uncle Rocco begrudgingly flew his brother's body back in from Chicago, to be with my grandmother and my father in Nassau Knolls.

One late afternoon with the sun still warm whenever the wind stopped blowing, I stood over my father's grave and I finally realized what the old man had been looking for all those hours seated at the back porch window.

Second chances.

Substitute teaching paid some bills for a while, twenty-five bucks a day, but I gave that up. I take labor jobs and send Annetta a couple bucks; she's given up asking me for more. I tried writing, got a few short pieces into local newspapers and specialty magazines.

I started book after book, but never finished one before this. I've changed some of the details here, I've moved the names around a bit, but basically I got it all down.

For a reason I can't remember, I brought home a bottle of Beefeaters gin on a hot summer afternoon. I never drink that stuff, can't stand any kind of clear booze at all.

I had worked my way halfway to the bottom of the bottle. As I was checking the fluid level against the clock, wondering if I would have to go out again, I remembered the half bottle of Beefeaters that Albert and I had buried at Jones Beach back in high school while wearing our Nickolai Lenin overcoats.

Driving the causeway to Parking Lot 4, I saw the obelisk of the water tower, rising like Washington's Monument out of the sand, then I looked over toward the inlet side of Jones Beach and I saw patches of cattails growing in the shallow, still water.

As kids, we didn't call them cattails. It was always called "punk." I don't know why. We'd find the stuff growing like mad, down in the Spinny Hill Swamp, out by the powerhouse.

We used to break off the heads, light up an end, and try to smoke them. The draw was harder than sucking water through a garden hose, the smoke was toxic and nauseating. Still, smoking punk had been the big fad one summer for us. Like so many things we did, we had no idea why we were doing it. Everybody else was doing the same thing. And, because punk-smoking had come to me so early and repulsive, I never smoked anything else except an occasional cigar to keep the bugs away.

I parked at the far end of the sprawling lot and I walked out over the dunes toward the ocean. At one point I realized that I could stand at a spot equidistance from where Arlynn had propositioned me in the West End dunes and where Albert and I had buried the booze.

I knew where I was going.

The sand felt cold on my hands because the sun wasn't hitting the ground there underneath the boardwalk. I dug. Then I dug again, a bit off to one side. Then again, a little off to the other side. I used my fingers as probes into the sand. I kept digging. People would walk above me, on the boards, and gaze down. I had long pants on.

I had never found Albert's grave, or Arlynn Svenson's grave, or any of the receptacles for Uncle Frank, departed husband of Naj Bimbaghulya. I had not found the grave of a dog or of a disinterred Indian.

But what I *did* find somehow, there in the sands of Jones Beach, at the far corner of the boardwalk, was that old bottle of Beefeaters gin. I really did.

The squared-off glass quart came stubbornly out of its burial place, still half full of the clear liquid. I brushed the sand off the label, off each of the glass sides. The sun was going down and as I held the bottle up, the red-orange sky made the booze look like a gin blossom.

There, reflecting in little auburn sparks of light and life, were many things for me to see. Yes, I was groggy by then, but still these things were there, reflected in the bottle that I was holding up.

We'd had a PBC basketball game the winter night that Buddy Holly, Richie Valens and the Big Bopper went down. The game went typically, with Eddie Neville sneaking himself onto the court as a sixth man and then slinking around in his Groucho Marx walk behind the ref's back when they stopped the game to count players. But afterwards, we found Tom Shevan and Herbie Schiltz fighting out in the alley, crying and kicking at each other.

If Albert Niklozak had died protecting me, then it was because he felt that I was a man who deserved protection. I did not have the right to contradict this man.

Arlynn had died asking me not to feel guilty, telling me that she did not love me. Albert had died asking me to save myself. Neither of these deaths deserved to be cheapened.

Thus, just like Buster Cook's stolen bottle of Chianti—the one that he took from us when we had him in for Thanksgiving turkey—that bottle of Beefeaters came out of the sand to be the post-mortem validation of the scenes of a life. The bottle of booze became my halo and my cross. Benny the Mutt would say, a relic of redemption.

Hours later, in the dark, I was still trying to finish it off. There was about an inch left in the bottle when I heard explosions up in the sky, and I turned and looked up to see streaks of light. Burning shards of reds and blue, yellow and green, floated down across the black.

The Marine Theater was shooting off its fireworks, across the inlet above Zak's Bay. I closed one eye, held up the bottle, and through it I viewed the gently moving colors in the sky. Back as a kid in Duck Alley, I had always wanted a kaleidoscope, I had asked for one every Christmas. The fireworks display went on for many minutes, and there was even a grand finale, just as there should be.

The facts of what had happened to us were clear to me, and they had been for awhile. I had understood it since I had listened to Arlynn's tape. But now, sitting in the sand, looking at fireworks filtered through glass and old gin, I seemed to be able to hook everything together in a different pattern, to view it from a different direction. A beatific vision.

The devil's stocking is knitted backwards, Nelson Algren's novels would tell you.

So I said "Thank you" to Cookie the bum. And I thanked Arlynn. I thanked Albert.

As I buried the bottle back into the sand beneath the boardwalk for a second time, a gust of wind chilled me, and I turned to look for my Nikolai Lenin overcoat.

I slept in the sand for the rest of the night.

The next morning on the ride back toward home from the beach, I pulled over and picked some punk. I used my pen and then a stick to punch a hole through the middle. And I lit up.

It stank and it burned my eyes and tongue; it was terrific. That punk left me woozy and validated.

"How sweetly did they float upon the wings of silence, through the empty-vaulted night."

— John Milton